# Afterthoughts

# Afterthoughts

## Lynn Tincher

Hydra
Publications

**Afterthoughts**
**The First Book in the Mind Bending Series**
Copyright © 2015 by Lynn Tincher
All rights reserved.

Fourth Edition

ISBN: 978-1942212218
ISBN:1942212216

Cover Art: John Tincher, Dark Palette Productions
Copyright – 2015 Lynn Tincher

Story Consultant: Peyton Skelton, Kilted Pictures

Hydra Publications
Goshen, KY 40026

www.hydrapublications.com

*For Emily, Aaron, Becca and Eric*

*Without you, this would not have been possible. I want to make you proud.*

*I love you all.*

# Acknowledgements

I would like to thank Terry, Laura, Cara, Tammy and Eric for your advice and editing abilities. Your belief in me keeps me going. I'd also like to thank Dave Mattingly from Blackwyrm Fiction for believing in me and publishing the Mind Bending Series.

A great big, huge thanks goes to Peyton Skelton for believing in this story and me. Thank you for your advice and story line development. You've made this adventure brand new. And thanks to Diane Musselman for working with Peyton to turn Afterthoughts into an amazing script! The movie will be amazing!

For all the rest of my friends, family, and the wonderful people I work with, thanks you. I really appreciate your passing the word along and keeping me strong.

# Afterthoughts

# Chapter 1

Detective Paige Aldridge pulled into her parking spot at the Louisville Metro Police Station. She turned off the car, closed her eyes and sighed. As she reached to gather her things together, her cell phone rang. "Oh Aileen," she whispered as she let it ring one more time.

Finally, she pushed the button to answer. "Hey, girlfriend!"

"Paige! How are you darlin'? Where are you right now? Is today the day you're going back in right? Seems like it still maybe a little early for you to be back on the job?" Aileen said without taking a breath.

Paige tried to find the opportunity to answer. "Yep. I am back to work today. It *has* been nearly two months since I was here full time. I need to be back here now. Get back to something normal." Paige looks at her fingernails in an attempt to keep her hands busy

"Well, I guess you have to go back sometime. Please take it easy today. Knowing how stubborn you are, you are probably..."

Paige cut her off, "...going to reopen Anthony's case today? Yes, I am! You know as well as I do that his son didn't kill him."

"Honey calm down. I on your side here. But, your very own boss, the Chief of Police, has closed the case. I loved your brother-in-law as much as you did, but, wouldn't it just be better to move on?"

"Do you really think Richie killed Anthony? The kid was troubled, but he loved his family! And I promised Sarah I would find the real killer! I... I wasn't there when she needed me... I know I could have done more!" Paige started to sob a little as she fought hard to keep it together. She looked around the outside of the car to be sure no one could see her.

Aileen tried to calm her down. "Listen this has been rough on all of us. You have been there. None of this is your fault. I think you should come over and we can get you some tea and."

"Aileen thank you but no, I have to get this started. I am the only one who can see this through. I know you mean well but I have to go in now. They are expecting me back on the job today. We will talk soon. I promise you."

"Paige! I think..." Too late. Paige hung up on her.

# Chapter 2

A huge crowd was gathered in the ballroom at the Galt House in Louisville, Kentucky. Banners of red, white and blue were meticulously hung everywhere; on tables, hanging from the ceiling. Nets full of balloons also hung overhead, waiting to be dropped.

Detective Paige Aldridge slowly walked toward the head table where her sister, Sarah, and her teenage nephew stood. Sarah looked as glamorous as usual while Richie looked like the suit would set him on fire. His gothic appearance was completely out of sorts in the blue suit and red tie. Paige smiled and hugged her sister while reaching for Richie's hand. He took it and half smiled. Paige swore he blushed a little. She secretly wished that Richie had not dyed his hair black. She missed his red mop.

A Wave 3 Newscaster stood to the side with the cameraman bustling around her, pulling at cords and fidgeting with his lights.

Paige's brother-in-law, Senator Anthony Steckler, walked to the head table as Sarah and Paige joined him.

The cameraman finally was situated and the light flashed on. The newscaster began. "And here's Senator Steckler, awaiting the final results. His fight against the local drug scene will probably be what carries him through according to the exit polls. Beside him is his sister-in-law, Detective Paige Aldridge. She's the youngest officer to be promoted to Detective in Louisville history. Her uncanny ability to understand the criminal mind will no doubt help the Senator's agenda. And to her right is the wife of Senator Steckler, Sarah. Sarah is a lead surgeon at University Hospital. Behind her is the Senator's son, Richard…"

Paige spotted her boyfriend, David, as he carefully made his way through the back of the room. She squeezed Sarah's arm as she left to meet him.

David kissed her cheek as she approached and whispered in her ear. "Paige, let Jay handle the stakeout tonight. You need to be here with the family."

"I am here with the family. But, if my partner needs me I will be there as soon as it's over. Who knows, tonight may be the night that the shit hits the fan."

"You need more time, Paige," he said as he grabbed her hand.

Paige pulled it away. "Time for what? To feel sorry for myself?" She stared back toward her family.

The Senator smiled at the crowd as he turned his back toward them to address Richie.

"Don't make a scene. I know you don't want me to be re-elected, but I'm certain I will be. You have to be on your best behavior." He said under his breath while leaning toward Richie.

Richie shuffled his feet then glared at his father. "Whatever! Maybe you shouldn't treat me like I'm five."

"I mean it. You can take your moody self right on home as soon as this is over. Until then, put a damn smile on your face, will ya?"

"You don't care about me. It's all about the *perfect* family for the public. Well, I hate to tell you this, but your family ain't perfect."

Suddenly, the results were in and balloons cascaded down into the ballroom. As Paige moved along to try to get to the head table, her phone rang.

"Jay, where are you?"

Her partner was on the other line, "You know where I am, I need you damn it!"

"Now?"

"No, wait until the zombie apocalypse. Of course now! It's all coming apart…"

"Okay, I will be there as soon as I can."

Paige hung up and reached the group just as Sarah also received a call.

She turned to the family just before they stepped up to the podium. "There's an emergency surgery that I need to get to. However, I have a few moments. They are prepping my patient now."

"I need to leave as well. There's a break in the case." Paige added.

Anthony nodded to them both as balloons continue to fall from the ceiling. Before anyone could get away, photographers force them all to bunch together for a family photo. With a determined face, Paige made a break for it waving goodbye. As she headed for the door, she almost knocked over a brunette woman who was watching from the sidelines.

"Oh, I'm so sorry," Paige said to her.

The woman turned and walked away without a word.

Sarah graciously excused herself from the room as Anthony positioned himself behind the podium to give his acceptance speech.

"I'm overwhelmed with being given the chance to continue the fight against Kentucky's growing drug problem…"

# Chapter 3

Paige's car screeched to a halt outside of a downtown building. She reached into the glove box and grabbed her gun. Exiting the car, she ran into the building like she's been there a hundred times before. She flipped the door open and sprinted up the stairs. As she got to door number 32, she paused to catch her breath then opened the door. She let out a whistle and entered. The room was totally dark.

As she closed the door she heard a gruff voice, "I am still not your dog!"

"Yeah, I know that. My dog actually listens to me, and I don't want to get shot... What the hell is happening now?"

Her partner of two years, Jay Vittadini, smiled while looking through binoculars at a room across the street. "Yeah you might have actually been on time for once... By the way did he win?"

"Yes, he did. The results came in then I bolted."

"Good that solves two problems. Now you can get back to being a detective full time and Senator Steckler can help clean up these asshole drug lords."

Paige walked across the room and stared at Jay as he was in full surveillance mode. He was all set up in a comfy chair, a tripod with a used, but still impressive zoom lensed camera on it and some sound equipment as well. Jay didn't stop watching through the binoculars.

"What's the sit rep?" she asked him.

"These guys are as good as locked up. I got plenty on them while you were out on the town. Rodriguez and Smith are on their way back with arrest warrants. You should get ready to go arrest some people. The deal went down I tell ya."

Jay handed Paige some headphones and the binoculars. "Here, you listen for a sec. I need to pee."

"Thanks for sharing, partner!"

"Oh, I am sorry! Did I offend your delicate sensibilities? *My most sincere pardon, your ladyship! I must go off to the powder room!*"

Paige laughed, "You jerk!"

She put on a bulletproof vest and flipped out her badge that hung on a necklace. She threw on the headphones and grabbed the binoculars.

She could see across the street. Two men were in a room having a heated discussion. One man, the one that appeared to be the head of the operation remained with his back to her. She couldn't get a good look at them.

"You will be responsible for distribution and collection in St. Matthews and Middletown, while we will continue to control Prospect and the eastern county."

"So it's pretty much the same deal as before?"

"No, your group has more responsibilities."

"And more risk! If that clown gets re-elected, then we will be more exposed while you get to sit back and rake in the cash."

"Well, I hate to break it to you but that clown was just re-elected and there wasn't a damn thing that went right to prevent it! So just get over it and get to work. If you don't like it, you can just leap off of the Sherman Minton..." he took a breath and paced the room. "What did I do wrong? How could this have gone this badly? Ah, I know what to do."

Suddenly, Paige closed her eyes. She envisioned that one man was shooting the other. She could see the gun drawn and the finger pull the trigger. She threw off the headphones and took off, leaving Jay behind. She flew down the stairs and ran across the street and didn't pause until she reached the door at the bottom of the stairs. As she placed her hand on the door just as a shot went off, knocking her back against a wall. She slowly fell to the street. She got a shot off as well, but missed, hitting the frame above the door. Both suspects pushed past her and ran down the street.

Jay's voice crackled over the radio. "Hey can't you wait for me? I heard gunfire. Are you okay?"

Paige slowly sat up, out of breath and pushed herself into a standing position. She was totally pissed off now.

She reached for her radio and pushed the button, "I'm fine. But get here quick. They are getting away."

"On my way! Backup is almost here."

The sounds of sirens filled the air. Paige sat down on the curbside and waited. When Jay showed up, she pointed him in the direction where they escaped. He took off but continued to look back at Paige. She waived him off to show she was okay.

Moments later, Jay returned empty handed to find Paige fighting off the other officers as they hovered over her to make sure she was all right. She refused their desperate pleas to get her to go to the hospital. However, she did allow the EMTs to get a look at her. As Jay made his way to her, the press arrived wanting pictures and asking questions. Jay pushed them away and pulled

Paige toward her car.

"My God, you were shot! Are you sure you are okay?" he asked her. "Maybe you should take some more time off? Ya know, deal with the added stress. You've been through…"

"Are you kidding me? I'm fine … Stress? You don't know about stress until you find out you're suffering from amnesia after being found in a friggin' ditch, half dead! This is cake!"

Jay wished he hadn't pissed her off. "All the more reason. You need to take more time and deal with that. It's only been a..."

"What do you know? I thought you were on my side. You sound like David."

Paige shoved Jay off and stormed to her car. Jay's mouth opened, trying to find a response. When none came, he tried to chase her down. Too late. She was in and started her engine before he could get to her.

# Chapter 4

Paige drove around for nearly an hour trying to blow off steam. She was sick and tired of everyone coddling her like a child and desperately wanted to get back to something normal even if that meant being shot. She stopped the car and laid her head on the steering wheel.

After only a moment, she dozed off. Her thoughts drifted to someone who was pacing around her. His presence surrounded her. She could feel his eyes boring holes right through. The feeling of suffocation took over and she fought to breathe. Paige felt hands on her throat. Her lungs felt like they were on fire!

Paige jolted awake, flung open the car door and threw up. As she collected herself, her phone rang. She could see it was Sarah.

"Hey, sis!" Paige answered.

"Oh my God, Paige. Anthony... he's dead." Sarah was half sobbing.

"What? What happened?"

"I've called 9-1-1. I came home from the hospital and he was lying on the bedroom floor. I couldn't... Oh my God, I couldn't save him. I couldn't bring him back to me!"

"Sarah, calm down. I'll be right there. I'm …" Paige looked around and realized she had stopped her car only a block away from Sarah's house. She could see several police cars had already arrived. "I'll be right there!"

Paige jumped out of the car and ran for the Stecklers' Estate. She pushed her way through the officers to get to the door. Richie grabbed her as soon as she made it.

Hysterical, he sobbed, "I was asleep. I was in my room the whole time. I was."

Paige was a bit disoriented, "I'm sorry. I know you were. I know you were." Before she could catch her breath, Sarah fell into both of their arms, sobbing uncontrollably.

Jay arrived on the scene. He scoured the crowd to locate Paige without any luck. He asked a few questions of the officers as he worked his way around the yard. Finally, Jay found Chief John Waters and headed into the garage to talk. "So, what do you know?"

Chief Waters looked at his notepad; "Sarah came home from the hospital this morning to find the Senator dead in the bedroom. It's all preliminary, but it looks like the Senator was killed by strangulation. We'll have to wait to find out for sure."

Jay nodded. "Have you seen Paige?"

"Yeah, she ran into the house a few minutes ago."

"Thanks," Jay said as he put his hand on Chief Waters' shoulder. "I'll go find her."

Jay worked his way into the house and up the stairs where the Senator's body was found. There he found Paige with a host of officers and FBI agents in tow. He watched as Paige methodically made her way around the body. She looked closely at his neck, just as if it were any other case. Careful not to touch anything, she made every effort to take in every single detail.

As she worked, one of the FBI agents watched from the corner. When he paced a bit, his shoe hit something on the floor. He looked down and found Paige's ID badge from the election party. Carefully, he picked it up while making sure no one else in the room had noticed and carefully placed it in his pocket.

Paige continued to stand over the body as the investigators took pictures, oblivious to the actions around her. She had yet to realize that Jay had entered the room. Unconsciously, her hand rubs her throat and she swallowed hard. Tears started to form in her eyes. Before she let them fall, she turned from the group. She caught sight of Jay and motioned for him to follow her.

Jay walked with her into the guest bedroom. "Paige, one of the neighbors came by. She said she heard Richie and Anthony arguing last night."

"So. They don't get along. What teenage boy gets along with his father?"

"True, but Richie was the only one home at the time of the murder."

"What are you saying?"

"Just prepping you. Right now, he's the last person to see Anthony alive."

Paige shook her head and stepped back out into the hallway. She ran down the stairs without stopping until she hit the front yard. Breathless, she surveyed the scene. By now, there was a huge mass of people that gathered around the estate; reporters, police, FBI, neighbors, and the woman she ran into at the election party. Paige frowned at the thought of recognizing her. However, she ran into the crowd of people. She felt like they were swirling around her, yet she managed to see someone slipping from view in the shadow of some trees. Paige fought her way toward them, chasing them on through the neighborhood until she reached her car. They were gone. *Who was that?*

# Chapter 5

Paige fought hard against nausea that was quickly consuming her. She leaned against the tree trunk of a huge oak that stood in her adopted sister's front yard. Her hands shook violently as she tried to cover her mouth. Her stomach gave another turn. Taking a deep breath, she stood up straight and squared her shoulders. Gathering up her remaining strength, she walked back toward the garage.

Unusually cold for a late August evening in Louisville, Kentucky, a soft breeze swirled around her; raising the hair on the back of her neck as her eyes made their way from the floor to the scene. Suicide. It's never easy to see. But her seventeen-year-old nephew? A boy she felt was as much her very own son. *Why?*

She clutched her hands to her chest to keep her heart from escaping and circled around the lifeless body that hung in front of her. Richie's face was already swollen and blue. The smell of death filled the garage. She swallowed hard, forcing down the lump in her throat as she cautiously stepped over the small stepladder that was kicked aside to accomplish the deed. Paige steadied herself by grabbing the elbow of a fellow officer and maneuvered between the others. Silence swept through the room as everyone watched her. An investigator's camera flashed just as tears filled her eyes. She fought back the urge to run home screaming as she slowly backed away and turned toward the garage door where her partner stood.

Jay didn't try to force a smile when she walked toward him. Instead, he offered her his handkerchief. "Hey, Paige," he half whispered. "You okay?"

"N ... no. I am never ready for anything like this," she replied as she took a deep breath, not noticing the light mist that formed. It was difficult to draw another breath in, like trying to blow up a new balloon. Hugging herself tightly to fend off the nausea and chills, she leaned against the garage doorframe beside Jay. "Have you talked with Sarah? Is she okay?"

"Yes, she's inside. Tom's with her," Jay sighed; scuffing his feet on the driveway as he mindlessly glanced at what was left of the sunset. "She's had to deal with so much lately," he said as he gently put his hand on Paige's shoulder and gave it a squeeze. "She needs you and if you need me, I'm right here. I mean it."

Paige couldn't feel his touch. "I know," she drew in another deep breath while she covered his hand with hers trying to reach for some sort of reality. "I'll go on in and talk to her," she could only whisper as she walked around the front of the red BMW parked in the driveway.

Pausing when she reached the end of the gray stone sidewalk, she leaned against the railing.

She absentmindedly ran her hand across the top of the shrubs that she and Sarah had planted. Paige's parents died when she was three and Sarah's mother and father had adopted her. They passed away several years later while both Paige and Sarah were in college.

They were not only sisters but best friends as well. How could she help her now? Again, she felt helpless. *"If only I had come out to see Sarah when I wanted to earlier, Richie may have been okay,"* she thought to herself. Tears burned the back of her eyelids again as she thought that maybe, just maybe, she could have prevented Richie from killing himself.

She remembered Richie playing in the back yard and picking dandy lions for her. He would run up to her with handfuls of the bright yellow flowers along with the grass and clover that had happened to grow alongside them. She wanted to once again touch his red hair and freckled nose as he would smile up at her and shower her with hugs and kisses.

Paige remembered the panic-stricken phone call from Sarah only thirty minutes earlier. "He's ... dead ... oh God ... he's dead!" was all that Paige could make out between Sarah's sobs.

"Who? Anthony?" Paige tried to ask calmly.

"No ... oh, God Paige ... it's Richie ... he's in the ..." Sarah's frantic words became impossible to understand between the sobs.

"Have you called 9-1-1? I'm on my way!" Paige threw the phone down and ran out of the door. When her car squealed onto Sarah's street in Gellendale Estates, the police were already there, lights flashing in unison with an ambulance in the yard.

The silhouette of someone hanging from the garage ceiling made her stop in her tracks as if she had been smacked in the face with a baseball bat.

Paige snapped back to reality when another detective brushed her arm as he passed. She realized she was still standing at the foot of the sidewalk, white knuckled on the railing.

She carefully moved toward the door. She could hear a voice in the back of her mind saying, *"Be calm Paige.*

*Everything will be fine. Just relax."*

As she opened one of the large double glass storm doors, she could hear Sarah's sobs echoing from the parlor. What was left of her heart shattered into a million pieces as she ran into the room. Sarah's face was as pallid as death itself. As she tried to stand and run to Paige, Sarah stumbled and fell back onto the couch; knocking the throw pillows into the floor.

"Sarah …" breathless, Paige ran to her. Their arms closed around each other as if hanging on for their very lives. "Sarah, I'm so sorry!" she tried to comfort her. Not knowing what to say, Paige sobbed along with her. She rocked her back and forth, letting Sarah rest completely in her arms like she was her own child. She stroked Sarah's long blonde hair, desperate to comfort her. Paige tried to embrace the pain that Sarah was feeling, but she only felt numb. How could anyone understand such grief? The tears fell down Paige's cheeks as if a faucet had been turned on inside her, but she didn't feel the tears. She wished she could feel the pain. How could she relieve some of it for Sarah? What could she possibly say to make things better? Fragile and helpless, Paige did the only thing she could do. She held onto Sarah as if she were her very life.

"Sarah, I don't know what to say or do. I'm sorry, so sorry."

Sarah nodded and hugged her tightly. Paige could feel her relax a little as Sarah's breathing slowed. Hope, Paige had hope.

Finally, Paige opened her eyes, lashes heavy with tears. Glancing up, she found Tom Miller, one of the policemen on the scene, standing over them. She hugged Sarah once more. "I'm going outside to talk with Tom for a minute. I'll be right back." Sarah's swollen eyes looked at her blankly. She nodded her head as Paige squeezed her hand. When Paige stood to walk with Tom, she asked another police officer to look after Sarah for a few minutes and she and Tom headed for the door.

When they stepped out onto the front porch, Tom looked out at the scene in the front yard. The news vans and reporters were swarming the investigators while they were taping off the scene. This was the second time in the same week there had been a tragedy at Senator Steckler's estate and the reporters were determined to have answers.

A crowd of spectators was also gathering around, shouting questions without concern.

"She found him ... she came home tonight, opened the garage door and saw him there," Tom whispered to Paige as he pulled her from the crowd. "I'm surprised the poor woman has any sanity left. She was at the station earlier asking questions about the Senator's murder. She swears Richie was innocent. Now, I'm not so sure." Tom sat down on the step shielding himself from the crowd with the shrubs that lined the porch.

"If Richie was guilty, we need to find out why," Paige sighed as she sat beside him. "Did he need money? Drugs? Did he hate his father enough to kill him? Was it an accident in the state he was in that night? I have to find the answers somehow. For Sarah's sake!" Paige's eyes filled with tears again. She wouldn't let them fall. Not anymore. She had to be the strong Detective now, not the sobby sister.

That was the only way she could help Sarah. Biting her lip, she stood up gracefully with what precious little strength remained and walked back into the house with Tom behind her.

Before she could enter the parlor, Tom whispered. "They are going to be removing the body any minute now. Maybe you should take Mrs. Steckler somewhere else in the house so that she doesn't see."

"Thanks, Tom. I will," she said as she laid her hand

on Tom's arm with a light touch that appeared to be out of concern but was more of trying to keep from falling down. She slowly turned and walked into the parlor to where Sarah was now laying on the sofa.

"Come on, Sarah. Let's go upstairs and clean you up a bit." Paige offered her hand to help Sarah stand. She nodded and walked with Paige toward the stairs. As they entered the bedroom, Paige suddenly felt ill again. Breaking into a sweat as nausea swept over her, she fought the urge to rush into the bathroom. *"I need to be strong for Sarah because she really needs me now,"* she told herself.

As Sarah was changing clothes and drying her face with a hand towel, Paige walked to the window and looked outside through the blinds.

The EMT's were pushing Richie's body, covered in a white sheet, into the ambulance. The memory of the same scene with Anthony's body caused Paige's stomach to lurch, yet again. As she watched the scenes unfold in the front yard, she saw someone in the shadows behind the tree line. Watching him as he moved from tree to tree along the back of the crowd, a suspicious feeling came over her. *"Relax Paige,"* a voice whispered. *"It's just a curious neighbor or a member of the press. No need to overreact this time."* Rubbing the back of her neck, she turned her back to the window.

As she glanced around the room, she noticed the pictures on the desk and dresser. She walked over and picked up a picture of Sarah and Anthony. They had their arms around each other and they were both smiling happily. As far as Paige knew, they had a nearly perfect marriage, even for a politician. Fighting off a little twinge of jealousy, Paige placed the picture carefully back on the dresser. She wondered if she would ever find happiness like that.

She made her way to the guest bathroom and splashed cold water on her face until she felt better. As she looked at herself in the mirror, she wondered what to do next. *"I have to figure out if Richie was guilty or if there is someone else. Did Richie kill himself for another reason?"* Then it hit her. The obvious question, "Has anyone found a suicide note?" she asked the reflection in the mirror.

Sarah was back in the bedroom when Paige came back in. Paige put her arm around her and led her back downstairs to face more detectives, suspicions, doubts, and tears. "I'll be back in a couple of minutes," she assured her and hugged her tightly. Leaving Sarah with Tom as they reached the parlor, she ran back outside to find Jay.

Before she could even ask the question, Jay had the answer. "We found a note. It doesn't make any sense but it's all we have," he said as he handed her a note that had already been sealed in an evidence bag.

Paige's hands shook as she took it from Jay and held it up to the porch light. She could barely make out the words on the letter through the plastic in the dim light of the garage.

> *Dear Mom,*
> *I'm sorry for all of the trouble I've caused you and Dad. I need help. I love you.*
> *Richie*

"I don't understand. This letter sounds like someone who is reaching out, not someone who is … about to …" Paige was trembling.

"Exactly," Jay cut her off. They looked at each other with complete understanding. They had been partners long enough to develop a sense of what each other was thinking. Paige likened it to a marriage where the couple could speak to each other without saying a word. Jay was not only her partner but her friend. One she argued with frequently but completely understood; even if she didn't agree.

The rest of the investigation went quickly. Perhaps it was because Paige was numb and could not concentrate. After taking Sarah to stay at her Cousin Aileen's farm, she decided to go home.

She poured herself a large gin and tonic with the juice of an entire large lime, crawled into bed and opened her journal.

> *"It's amazing how quickly things can change. You think everything is normal, fine, routine. I mean, one minute I'm running bath water, ready to relax and the next, I'm staring death in the face. Why Richie? Why did he have to kill himself?"*

She sighed and continued to write in her journal as suggested by her psychiatrist.

> *"I feel as if my world is caving in on me. I'm getting smaller and smaller. I have no control anymore. I want to reach out and help, but I can't. I'm helpless, alone, insignificant."*

She toyed with the corner of the page as she put her pen in her mouth, tears streaming down her face. She wiped them on her sleeve, took the pen and continued.

> *"I feel like I'm going crazy. I can't*

*remember things, days even. Something is happening to me. I thought I was better. I thought I had made progress. Today, I started to visit my sister, Sarah, to check up on her and it was like a voice was telling me to leave her alone. So, I didn't call. I didn't call!"*

She drew several underlines.

*"I'm going out of my mind. I should have been there. If I had, Richie would still be alive!"*

She gave up, slammed her journal closed and turned off her light. She sobbed herself to sleep.

# Chapter 6

As morning broke, the bright sun streaked through the blinds onto Paige's bed. Her swollen eyes blinked as they adjusted to the light. She calmly watched the dust float through each streak of sunlight until the memories of the previous day invaded the stillness. Trying to put the vision of Richie out of her head, she decided to get up and make coffee. She sat on the side of the bed for a moment and ran her hand through the sunlight. Watching the streaked light dance across her arm and hand she thought, *"Such a simple pleasure."* One, she decided, she would never to take for granted again. Life is too precious and she had seen enough over the last year to make her appreciate what little things she had been blessed with.

Suddenly, a vision formed in her mind like a dream. She could see a small amount of light slicing the cold darkness of a small room. The window appeared to be boarded, but the strands of light still fought their way through, streaked across the room, and fell across her lap.

She felt a wave of nausea.

22

Holding on to the side of her bed, she shook her head, *"What the hell was that all about?"*

She shook her head again as if shaking out cobwebs. *"Coffee,"* she reminded herself and stood up to pull on her pink silk robe that lay casually across a huge overstuffed chair.

Harry, Paige's Labrador, looked up at her hopefully. She reached down and rubbed his soft, black ears. "I guess you need out."

He wagged his tail happily.

As she crept toward the kitchen, she rubbed her eyes, ran both hands through her long brown hair and rubbed her stiff neck. Harry pounced along beside her, happy to be up and about. "A nice, long, hot bath is just what I need," she whispered to herself as she opened the door and Harry bounded outside. She crossed to the counter and scooped coffee into the filter.

As the coffee brewed, she stepped back outside to pick up the paper. Instead of opening it, she tossed it on the kitchen table, afraid to look at the front page. She knew in her gut that the suicide of the late Senator's son would be front-page news and at that, she decided not to turn on the television. Rolling her head from side to side, she walked over to the phone on the kitchen wall, took it off the hook and laid it on the counter. She had already turned off her cell phone the night before. She knew that Sarah was with Aileen and would be fine.

With a deep sigh, she paced the floor, thinking.

Paige remembered when Anthony approached her in college to talk to her about Sarah. "I'm crazy about her, Paige. Do you think she'd marry me?" he asked her with his big handsome smile. Paige could tell he was nervous about asking her this question.

Paige tried to smile at him even though she was a little jealous.

"She'll say yes in a heartbeat. The two of you are

made for each other. I wish I could find what you guys have."

Anthony gave her a big hug, "Sarah's lucky to have you. She loves you, ya know."

"Thanks. I love her too," Paige gave him another hug, smiling.

Paige thought of Richie's letter as she shuffled into the bathroom to draw a bath. She added her favorite vanilla scented bath salts and lit all the candles that lined the garden tub. This was the way Paige knew she could think best. She loved to soak in a warm tub, surrounded with subtle light and wonderful scents. This was the only pampering she did for herself. She enjoyed a simple life with simple things. She didn't fuss over her hair or make-up and her furniture and apartment were plain and not cluttered. Harry was her only personal responsibility and if he had thumbs, he could let himself out. *Hmmm, maybe I'll get a doggie door.*

As the tub was filled, she returned to the kitchen to pour her coffee. *"A little coffee with my cream and sugar,"* she tried to laugh at herself as she poured most of a container of half-n-half in her cup. She looked out of the window and saw her neighbor walking the little Norfolk Terrier she brought home the month before. *"Amazing,"* she thought to herself, watching Jeanne go back into her house with the little dog and noticing that they both had short spiky orange hair. *"They've only been together a month and they already look alike."* Paige wondered if she and Harry looked alike somehow.

She smiled again as she headed back to the kitchen door to let Harry in. After locking the door, she walked to the bathroom, slipped off her robe and gown and lowered herself into the hot water until only her face was visible through the bubbles. She let the warmth of the water surround her and soothe her. She tried not to think of the day before, but the vision of Richie hanging from the rafters kept creeping back into her thoughts. *"Be calm Paige. Don't think about it. Everything is fine. Forget it,"* she kept hearing a voice say over and over. She sipped her coffee as she soaked in the warm tub, trying to let the sensations relax her mind.

Suddenly, she fought off the urge to forget it. She tried to think of Sarah and what she needed to do to help her. She had to figure out what was going on with Richie. Why he did what he did to himself? Tears poured down her cheeks as she realized she still had no answers.

She remembered how Sarah had been there for her in the past. Sarah hadn't done anything special other than listening when Paige needed to talk, or to giving her the space she needed when she didn't want to.

She smiled as she tried to remember the fun the two of them had getting to know each other growing up. She remembered when they skipped school shopped in the malls all day. They came home later with the beer they managed to convince a local storeowner to sell them. How stupid they must have looked snickering as they walked up and down the halls of their childhood home, trying not to look drunk. As she smiled to herself, she fell sound asleep.

A half hour later, she woke up shivering. Most of the water had drained out of the tub leaving her cold and damp. After considering running more hot water, she decided to get out instead. Before she could dry off, there was a frantic knock on the door and she could hear her boyfriend, David, scream, "Paige, you alright?"

"I'm fine ... I'm coming," she yelled trying to outdo Harry's barks. She threw on her robe and ran for the door.

When the door opened, David pulled her into his arms. "When I couldn't reach you, I got really worried. I had to come and check on you," he kissed her wet hair.

"I'm sorry. I just needed some time," Paige said as she automatically slid into his arms. She had to admit, it felt good to be held.

Harry must have felt the same way as he jumped up on them and tried to squeeze his way into the middle.

"I understand, baby," David whispered in her ear. He loosened his grip on her so he could pet the dog. "Come here you big goof!" He wrestled him around for a bit before grabbing Paige's hand and leading her into the living room to sit on the couch. "How are you holding up?"

Paige raised her head to look at him. "I'm okay. It's Sarah I'm worried about. She's lost both Anthony and Richie in less than a week, and then to deal with the possibility that Richie murdered his own father. I just can't even begin to imagine!" Beyond her control, the tears finally fell down her cheeks. "I need to go put on some clothes. I'll be right back." Paige walked quickly from the room leaving David to sit on the couch. Harry nudged his hand and David rubbed his ears softly.

"She's not doing very well," he whispered to Harry as he scratched behind one of his ears. "We're going to have to keep an eye on her."

She returned wearing a pink sweat suit. David picked up the conversation that Paige had hoped to avoid just a little bit longer.

"You've been dealing with it too, Paige. You were the one that put the pieces together leading to Richie murdering his father. Killing himself only proves his guilt." David hugged her again allowing Paige's tears to soak his shoulder. He then took a tissue from a box on the coffee table and handed it to her.

"I still don't think Richie killed Anthony," she paused. "How do you go on after something like this? I'm not sure I could!" She pulled back and looked at him. His dark blonde hair looked as if he had just jumped out of the bed. "I'm glad you're here. I thought I wanted to be alone. I was wrong." She tried to smile at him but ended up burying her face in the tissue.

"Where else in the world would I be?" He smiled at her, kissed her on the forehead, and touched her cheek. "You've faced your fair share and look at you now. Have you eaten?" He took her hand in his and caressed her fingers.

"No. I had a cup coffee, but it's cold now. There's more in the pot. Do you want some?" She started for the kitchen.

He pulled her back toward the sofa. "You just sit here and try to relax. I'll take care of the coffee. Breakfast too." He held both of her hands briefly before he turned and walked to the kitchen.

Paige wanted to resist but gave up. She leaned back in the sofa, grabbed her throw pillow, and hugged it tightly. She pulled her feet up under her and stared out of the living room window at the trees in her front yard.

David watched her from the door and noticed how her long brown hair fell over her shoulder and across the pillow she had pulled up in front of her. *"She is beautiful. Even after all she's been through, she is still beautiful,"* he thought to himself as he turned slowly and headed toward the kitchen.

She watched the blue jays playfully darting in and out of the branches and landing on her bird feeder. She couldn't remember the last time she put seeds in the damn thing. *"The poor things would starve if they had to depend on me,"* she thought to herself. The birds swept down over a small squirrel that was scratching around under the feeder causing the squirrel to run into the row of shrubs along the yard. *"If the squirrel would only figure out that he's bigger,"* she chuckled to herself.

She could hear David banging around in the kitchen

and wondered what he could be finding for breakfast. *"Hmmm, groceries, that's another thing I can't remember the last time I did."* Paige barely even had time to spend with David, yet here he was, making breakfast and worrying about her. *"I've got to spend more time doing things for me,"* she promised herself that this would also include time for David and Sarah. The tears began to flow again and she buried her face in the pillow. *"When will I ever run out of tears?"*

A few minutes later, David walked in carrying a tray with oatmeal, toast, and coffee. "I'm sorry. This was all I could find, and it's instant oatmeal at that," he smiled as he sat the tray on the coffee table.

"It's perfect," she smiled back as she took the tray and placed it on her lap. She picked up the spoon and pushed the oatmeal around in the bowl for a few seconds before she decided to take a bite of toast.

As she picked at her breakfast in silence, David watched her. Harry watched her as well, hoping she would carelessly drop a nibble. He took his nose and nudged her leg. Absentmindedly, Paige rubbed his head. With a large sigh and a low groan of disappointment, Harry lay down on the floor next to her.

David noticed her slim hands as she played with the spoon. *"Definitely not the hands of a cop,"* he told himself as he admired her. He felt his cell phone vibrating in his pocket and ignored it as he watched her try to eat. He thought she resembled a wet cat. Long and thin. He smiled when he realized she didn't eat the oatmeal and barely nibbled on her toast. When he saw her snub the coffee he remembered, "You need more cream and sugar, don't you?"

She smiled at him and begged, "Please?"

He took the cup from her and headed toward the kitchen, accepting the fact that she would not eat the oatmeal. Paige slipped the rest of her toast to Harry, who practically swallowed it whole.

When he returned, she had already placed the tray on the table with only the toast gone. "Guess you're not hungry?" he asked her as he handed the cup to her.

She shook her head and sipped the coffee. "This is all I need." She wrapped her hand around the cup and took another sip as she pulled her legs back up under her. "Thanks for taking care of me," she finally said.

"Like I said, where else would I be?"

"I'm sure you could come up with at least a hundred things you'd rather be doing," Paige said as she tried to sound light.

"When will you ever believe me?" he asked as he exaggerated his sigh.

"Probably never," she smiled halfheartedly. "Who would want to be with a cop that never has time for anything but being a cop? I know I wouldn't." Paige turned toward the window and continued watching the birds.

David sat next to her on the couch and took the cup from her hand. "I wouldn't be here if I didn't want to be. You know that." He started rubbing her neck. She tried to relax feeling his hands caress and squeeze her shoulders as she rolled her head around. It felt nice.

She didn't realize just how tense she was. He slowly rubbed her neck, hitting all of the tight spots and giving them an extra squeeze. It was painful, she realized, but at the same time it was a great relief. She leaned back into his arms and let him hug her tightly.

Paige could feel his cell phone vibrating in his pocket. She knew he was ignoring it. "You better get that."

"I'll call them back. You're more important," he whispered as he leaned forward and kissed her neck softly.

"Why do you put up with me?" she asked him as she

slowly turned toward him.

"Because I have to," he smiled and started kissing her ear. She whimpered softly as his lips made their way from her ear to her neck, his hands running up and down her arms. She let herself go in his caress, wanting to melt away with him. Feeling herself drift away in the sensations, she turned toward him to let him kiss her lips. His kiss was soft and gentle.

Paige opened her eyes and glanced back out of the window. She could see someone standing in the shadows of the trees. She jumped and ran toward the window.

"What is it?" David asked as he stood behind her.

"There, in the trees," she pointed. "There was a man, standing there.

I didn't see where he went, but it looked like he was watching us."

"I don't see anyone," David said as he looked across the yard.

"Whoever it was is gone now and I'm sure he couldn't see in through the window in this light."

"I'm going out to find him," Paige started toward the door.

"Paige, wait. There's no one there." David grabbed her arm, keeping her from running outside.

Paige whirled about on her heals. "He was there. I saw him!" she screamed at him.

"I believe you, but he's not there now. It's okay," he rubbed her shoulders, trying to calm her down.

"You're right," Paige forced a smile and stepped away from him.

"I'm sorry. I didn't mean to yell."

"That's okay, Paige, really," he pulled her into his arms and kissed the top of her head. "Sit down and drink your coffee."

Reluctantly, she obeyed, not taking her eyes off of the tree line.

Nothing else seemed amiss. The birds were still in search of seed and the squirrel was brave enough to come back out and forage below. *"I must be seeing things,"* she thought to herself as she picked the coffee back up to take another drink. Instead of a sip, she downed the entire cup.

# Chapter 7

The next three days passed quickly. Paige stayed with Sarah at Aileen's.

She busied herself helping Aileen care for Sarah, cooking meals, and forcing her to eat them. They made all of the funeral arrangements with only nods of agreement from Sarah, who hardly spoke a word and rarely acknowledged anyone who was speaking to her. It was obvious that she was just simply functioning and was getting worse by the day.

Paige wondered if she should suggest to Aileen that Sarah needed counseling. She thought about talking to the therapist who had helped her so much over the past year. Paige was sure he could help.

As Paige cleared the table from lunch, she remembered when Sarah had found her husband. She was adamant that someone broke into the house and strangled Anthony even though there was no sign of a break-in. Nothing was taken from the house and there was not a shred of DNA evidence to be found. There was only their son, Richard. Sarah told Paige on several occasions that Anthony argued with Richie about the drugs and alcohol. Some of the arguments became violent enough that things were thrown and items around the house were broken but they never actually hit each other. Sarah believed with all of her heart that neither of them would ever hurt the other physically.

When Paige questioned Richie, he didn't seem upset about his father's death. He even claimed to be in the house at the time of the murder but said that he didn't hear or see anything. *"How could he in the state he was in?"* Paige thought to herself remembering that he was totally inebriated that night. She thought about how sad it was that the sweet little-freckled face boy had become so messed up. He was a great kid; willing to give you the shirt off his back if he thought you needed or wanted it. Smiling all the time, he was absolutely full of life. She remembered all of the practical jokes he played on his dad.

At the end of his eight grade year, he had covered the door handle of Anthony's BMW with Vaseline. He laughed so hard that he rolled across the front yard while watching Anthony try to figure out what was wrong with the door. Anthony never did figure it out until Richie finally told him about a year later, when he felt he was safe from being grounded from his video games.

Paige was loading the dishes into the dishwasher when Aileen walked in.

"I'll stay again tonight so we can get Sarah ready for the funeral in the morning," Paige said softly.

"Thank you, Paige. You have been a true godsend." Aileen hugged her tightly.

"I just need to run home to pick up a few things after we get her settled down tonight." Paige sighed, cleared her throat, and paused for a moment before she said, "I know a great therapist. I'm sure he would be glad to see Sarah. Do you think we can get her to go?"

"I think we have to force her to," Aileen responded,

making Paige feel relieved for making the suggestion. "I don't think she can cope with all of this. At least when Anthony died, she was occupied for a few days with trying to find his killer. I think this took what was left of her." Aileen wrung the dishtowel between her hands.

"I'll give him a call this afternoon. I'm sure he will see her right away." Paige hugged her. "I just wish there was something I could do to make this all go away. I will promise you this; I will get to the bottom of it all. That's the only way Sarah will have any peace."

Paige finished helping Aileen clean up the kitchen then walked to Sarah's bedroom to check on her. Sarah was sitting in a chair by the window, looking out. Paige watched her as she stared, not moving, barely breathing. *"What's going on in her head?"* Paige wondered.

Sarah was there for Paige just over a year ago. Paige had disappeared.

After missing for two months, she was found in a ditch fifteen miles outside of Louisville, Kentucky, only five miles away from Paige's home.

She was starved, beaten, and dirty with no memory of anything—not even the past day. Sarah had taken Paige into her home and over the next year, nursed her back to health. Sarah worked hard to gain Paige's trust and friendship and tried desperately to help her remember her life. With counseling and time, Paige began to remember her past with one exception. She could not remember the two months when she had been kidnapped. It didn't matter what therapy techniques were used. Dr. Southerland tried hypnosis and talked to her about things that could have possibly happened to her during her disappearance.

As much as Paige wanted to try to remember, she couldn't. The only thing she was sure of was that she had been severely abused. Her wrists and ankles had deep rope burns and her face was bruised and swollen

almost past recognition when she was found.

She decided that it was probably better not to remember anything except the love and friendship Sarah had given her. They were best friends. More like sisters than true sisters could ever be. She wondered what she could do to even begin to return the favor. Could Sarah forget the pain and go on? She couldn't see how.

Paige walked over to the window and knelt down in front of Sarah.

She picked the afghan up out of the floor and placed it back in Sarah's lap. She took Sarah's face in her hand and looked her in the eyes. Her pale blue eyes didn't respond.

"Sarah, I'm here. I'll always be here for you. I love you!" There was only a faint smile from Sarah. "Remember being there for me, Sarah?

Remember all of the crying sessions? Remember all of the fights over which of us liked Andy Smith the most? Gee, we were nuts over that guy. But he was the most gorgeous thing in High School!" She smiled and squeezed Sarah's hand. She saw Sarah's eyes light up and make contact, but only for a moment. Sarah wasn't completely gone yet.

There was hope. "Do you remember the night you were out with Sam and I had to cover for you?" Paige forced a laugh. "I told Mom that I had just left you at the mall when you were really in Sam's car?" Sarah turned her head back toward the window.

With a small sigh of defeat, Paige sat down in the chair opposite from Sarah and glanced out of the window. She could see the beautiful fields lined with perfect black fences and horses grazing lazily in the sunshine. "Wouldn't it be wonderful if your only cares in the world were which spot of grass to eat next?" Paige half whispered. She could see Harry exploring the fence line and chasing a rabbit that had been disturbed by his presence. He really enjoyed being on the farm. Watching out of the window for a few moments longer, she saw someone duck behind the barn. She strained to see who it was. Harry seemed unaware of the intruder. She dismissed the thought. *"Maybe it was just a worker,"* she tried to convince herself as she watched from the window. Finally giving up, she hugged Sarah tightly, kissed her on the cheek, and promised to come back and sit with her for a while later in the afternoon.

Paige left the room and walked out to the front porch swing. She pulled her cell phone out of her pocket and called Dr. Southerland to set up an appointment for next week. When he agreed, she closed her phone and glanced out at the farm. She watched the trees sway in the breeze. The darkening sky warned of an approaching storm and she listened to the thunder in the background. The weather had warmed considerably since the night Richie killed himself.

She looked out over the rolling fields of Aileen and Jones Childers' horse farm. "Such a beautiful place, totally at peace with the world. It's hard to believe this farm is so close to the city," Paige said to Aileen as she stepped onto the front porch, carrying two tall glasses of iced tea.

"Thank you," she said as she took a glass from Aileen's hand.

"We love it out here. It's a lot of work, but when you sit on this porch and look around, it makes it all worth it." Aileen joined her on the swing. "During the Derby it gets a little crazy, though. Everyone is busy mowing and planting flowers and shrubs. But when the farm is in tip-top shape for all of the visitors, it's just like a movie. We are so proud of this place. We have a lot of fantastic people working here."

"I can only imagine! I'd like to come out here in the spring and see what it's like then," she smiled at Aileen and took a long drink of her tea. She looked around at all of the beautiful landscaping. Paige could only imagine how magnificent the long driveway must be in early spring. It was lined with Bradford Pear trees on both sides with Dogwood trees lining the fence that ran parallel with the driveway.

Scattered beneath the trees were begonias of every imaginable color planted so they looked like stained glass windows along the way. The edges of the begonias were lined with bright yellow marigolds that seemed to breathe the sunshine all the way down the drive. This all led up to a glorious statue of a thoroughbred and its groomer. The groomer was holding a curry comb in one hand and a hose in the other that had water cascading over the back of the horse to land in a beautiful pool teeming with koi. Paige fought back the urge to get up and walk over to the statue. She wanted desperately to run her hand through the water and watch it as it ran down her arm. She imagined her hands filling up and water spilling over as she cupped them under the hose.

Her hands ... she remembered them tightly gripping around his neck.

*"No!"* a voice screamed from inside her causing her to jump just as lighting flashed in the distance.

Trying to gather her thoughts, Paige sat in silence for a few moments, watching the storm creep closer and feeling the breeze pick up. They watched as the horses in the fields started running around, excited by the upcoming weather. The workers were busy trying to bring them to the barn and put away their equipment. Harry ran to the house quickly and lay down on the woven welcome mat at the front of the door.

"How are you, Paige?" Aileen asked quietly, breaking Paige's trance.

"I'm as good as can be expected, I guess. I just wish I could help Sarah. I don't have a clue what to say or do.

If only I could make it all go away for her. Bring them back somehow. I can't even figure out what's happened," Paige said helplessly, trying to ignore the vision she had just had.

*"What did that mean?"* she asked herself. *"Why were my hands around Anthony's throat?"*

"Just being here for her is enough right now. She knows you're here and that she's not alone." Aileen placed her hand on Paige's arm as a small blue Corvette started up the driveway toward the house. Paige recognized Jay's car. Wanting to step away from Aileen and clear her head, she stood to walk toward the drive.

She was waiting as Jay parked and climbed out of the car. "Howdy partner!" he nodded in her direction, pretending to tip his nonexistent cowboy hat.

"Hey there you! Mighty long drive you took to come see little ole me!" Paige said with an exaggerated southern drawl and batting her eyelashes. She felt good teasing with Jay this way. It was the first time she genuinely smiled in days. "What's up?" she said, as she was suddenly afraid the conversation was about to get serious.

"I just wanted to come out and check on you guys. See how things are going and if you need any help with anything." He walked around the side of the car to stand by her.

Paige was so glad to see his handsome face and to know that he was there as a friend, not a detective. "It's going … I'm really worried about Sarah," she said, quickly avoiding any conversation about herself.

"Aileen and I were talking about sending her to Dr. Southerland. I've made an appointment for her next week. She barely exists. She doesn't eat or talk. We have to force her to clean up and go to bed. I think she'd wither away sitting in that chair by the window." Paige pointed to the window where Sarah was sitting.

"I'm so sorry, Paige. I hate to see you all going through this." Jay pulled her into his arms and gave her a soft hug. "I'm here if you need me."

"Thank you. That means so much." She started to hug him tighter just as a loud *boom* rang out as lightning struck a tree less than a half-mile away. "Come on, we better get inside." She grabbed his arm and pulled him toward the house. As she started to move, her head began to spin. Flashes of light and images began to rush through her mind.

She could see herself in a dark room where she could only see one small, boarded window that had light only as lightning flashed outside.

She was frozen still. Bound by something she didn't understand. Terror overtook her. "I can't move!" she screamed. She could feel someone hit her across her face. The pain overtook her senses and her head began to spin. She could feel someone standing over her and could hear a slow, deliberate laugh.

Then she collapsed. Jay caught her in his arms before she could hit the ground. "Paige, are you okay?" He scooped her into his arms and carried her toward the house.

Aileen, who was still sitting on the porch swing, saw everything.

She rushed to help Jay get her inside and lay her on the sofa. As she ran to get a damp towel and a glass of water, Jay rubbed Paige's arm and squeezed her hand. "Come on Paige, talk to me … Talk to me!"

When Paige gained consciousness, she found Jay leaning over her, stroking her hair. "Feeling better?"

"What happened?" she asked nervously, feeling as if her head would explode along with the thunder crashing outside. She reached up to rub her temples.

"I don't know. You just fainted." Jay handed her the washcloth which she gratefully took and washed her face with it.

Paige rubbed her head for a moment and began to remember her vision. She told him about everything she could remember about the window, being hit, the laugh, and the lightning.

Paige started to talk. "I wonder if I … could I be?" She began to tremble.

"Do you think you are remembering those months, Paige?" he questioned as he took her hand. "Do you think you could have been locked away in a room like that? Did you recognize the laugh?"

"I don't know. All I know right now is that I need a glass of water."

She slowly sat up on the edge of the couch taking the glass Jay had in his other hand. After a good long drink she said, "If I were in a room like that, I don't want to remember it." Paige stood. With shaky knees, she walked toward the large picture window in the living room and watched the storm raging on outside.

She thought about how different the farm looked now. It was no longer warm and inviting but cold and volatile. She hated to think of the beating all of the beautiful flowers were taking now and wondered what it would take to clean up after such a storm on a farm this size.

She could see that tree branches were littered all across the once beautiful fields.

Jay walked up behind her and put his arm around her shoulders.

They stood in silence, watching the storm while Paige allowed herself to lean on him for support. She normally wouldn't allow herself to lean on anyone; even metaphorically. She wanted to be independent and strong. She didn't want to be unstable or afraid, yet that was exactly the way she felt.

Harry walked up beside her and put his head under

her hand. She rubbed his ears, realizing what a great comfort the dog had been for her. He was her baby and he would protect her to his death if he had to. Paige would do the same for him. She bent down and hugged her big buddy tightly. He licked her face and all of her fears seem to melt away. Paige understood that Harry loved her unconditionally. *"Too bad people don't seem to be able to feel that way,"* she thought to herself.

"Wish I had a dog like you," Jay told Harry as he bent down to aid in the scratching. Of course, Harry was happy with all of the attention and his tail thumped the floor loudly. Paige glanced at Jay and caught his eyes for a moment. Uneasy with the situation, she turned her head toward Harry and kissed the top of his head.

"I don't know what I would have done without him. He's helped keep me going every day." Continuing to avoid his gaze, she stood and turned back toward the window. "I think it may let up soon," she said as the wind seemed to die down and the thunder sounded more distant.

"I hope so. That was a doozie," he tried to laugh and sound light hearted.

Paige felt him put his hand in the small of her back, sending a soft chill up her spine. She paused her thoughts long enough to realize that she had too many emotions running through her right now. She needed time to sort them all out before she could begin to understand them.

"Would you excuse me for a bit? I would like to go lie down," she half whispered to Jay as she turned toward him.

"Sure, I'll be here for a while. I'd like to visit with Sarah a little."

Smiling halfheartedly, she turned and walked toward her room. She paused long enough to say thank you, without looking at him.

When Paige reached the guest bedroom in which she was staying, she sat on the bed, half in tears, and pulled out her journal.

> *"There's something going on with me. I'm seeing things, memories that I don't want to remember. Maybe they aren't memories.*
>
> *Maybe my mind is making them up. I feel like there are so many things going on inside that it's like I have tiny little arrows, poking at me from all directions. I don't know what to do, where to turn, how to feel, or what to believe. I long to be touched, but David is not here. Jay touched me today and I reacted. It was an innocent thing, but I reacted. I am so confused. I can't help Sarah.*
>
> *I don't know what to say to her and I'm frustrated. I hate seeing her like this."*
>
> *"Today, I saw the room again. I couldn't move. I was trapped. Someone hit me in the face. What does that mean? I heard someone laugh. Who was it? It sounded like a man. I also saw my hands.*
>
> *I can't even finish that thought right now. I don't want to admit what I saw. What's going on with me?"*

Tears fell down her cheeks as she slammed the journal shut.

Determined not to face any more right now, she lay on the bed and closed her eyes.

# Chapter 8

Jay spent the rest of the afternoon with them and Aileen asked him to stay for dinner. "That way, you can take Paige home to get her things for the funeral and bring her back. I'm worried about her being out on her own, especially in this weather!"

"For goodness sakes! I'm a cop! I think I can handle a storm! It's over anyway," Paige argued.

"That's not the point. You don't need to be alone right now. I'm fine with Sarah," Aileen fussed at her in a motherly way, pushing Paige's hair behind her ears. "I'll get her ready for dinner."

"I agree with Aileen," Jay chimed in as he brushed his brown hair back off of his forehead and scratched behind his ear. "I'm not sure you need to be driving right now."

"I guess I'm outnumbered then," Paige said defeated. "I guess that means you'll stay for dinner." She could see Jay's face light up. His deep brown eyes seemed to glow. At least Paige knew that he genuinely wanted to be there. Knowing this made Paige feel strangely happy and less of a burden.

"Come on, we'll go get your things before Aileen gets dinner on the table." Jay held out his arm to lead Paige toward the door.

"Okay, okay. But don't get used to taking care of me. I won't let you for too long," she smiled as she reluctantly took Jay's arm. Harry ran around their legs, begging to go too. "You have to stay, sweetie. There's only enough room in Jay's car for two." Harry's ears lowered and his tail dropped. Making three turns, he lay down on the floor. "I'll be right back. I promise," she smiled and pat his head as they turned to walk out toward the Corvette.

They drove in silence for a while. Jay was giving her time to think and sort things out. He didn't know what to do or say to help or comfort her, even though he desperately wanted to. He thought about reaching over to hold her hand, but a cell phone ring interrupted his thoughts.

"Hello?" Paige answered after digging through her purse to find the phone. "Yea, I'm fine … I'm heading home to get some things and then heading back to Aileen's … Will I see you tomorrow? … I see … I will … Thanks for calling to check on me … Bye now." She hung up with a huge sigh. She looked up at Jay, who was pretending not to listen. "That was David. He'll be in Minneapolis on business tomorrow."

"I'm sorry, Paige. I'm sure he will be thinking of you while he's gone and wishing he were here."

"Yeah, he has a book signing that he can't miss." Somehow Paige felt as if she were making excuses for him and wondered if Jay picked up on that.

The storm was over when they returned to the Childers' farm. Aileen insisted that Jay took Paige for a walk around the farm to let her get some fresh air before dinner. Harry, of course, happily agreed to go along.

"This place is incredibly beautiful," Jay announced as

they walked toward the horse barn. Paige wanted to avoid the fountain now.

"Yes, it is. I can't wait to see it in the spring. Aileen says it's beautiful when they have it all ready for the Derby. I'll bet that's something to see." Paige wandered along the fence line, touching the leaves of the Dogwood trees as she went, feeling the water trickle down her fingers from the leftover rain.

"I'm sure." Jay wasn't paying as much attention to the trees as he was watching her enjoy them. Suddenly he was whacked in the face with a rain-drenched branch that Paige had purposely sent his way.

"You'll pay for that!" he chased her toward the barn.

Breathless, they ran down the way in between the stalls. They were greeted with the warm smell of fresh hay and horses. They walked along, stall to stall, petting the noses of the thoroughbreds that would allow them to as the horses were eating from their feedbags hanging in the stalls. The barn was warm and dry, nothing like the storm-drenched fields outside. Paige was glad to be in such an inviting place.

It comforted her somehow.

"It's amazing how soft their noses are," Paige said as she rubbed her knuckles across the nose of a chestnut mare. "And some of their names are so interesting. This one is called Snacks R on Us. See, it's on the brass tag on the harness." Paige tried to turn the horse's harness toward Jay so he could see the tag. The horse shook her head to fight her off.

Jay laughed. "I hope they're not referring to dog food."

Paige had to laugh along with him. "At least his name is not Glue Stick!"

"Hey, this one is Sexy Jay," Jay chuckled as he reached for the harness of the horse in the next stall.

"Let me see." Paige hurried to the horse's stall. "You

big goofball!" she laughed as she shoved him to the side. The horse was Big N Da Saddle.

They walked back to the house laughing and coming up with their own silly horse names like 'Turn the Paige' and 'Jay It Out Loud'. Paige did feel better; better than she had in weeks.

She picked up a stick that had been blown out of a tree and threw it for Harry to fetch. He chased it down and brought it back to her. They took turns throwing it for him. "He would love to live out here where he could run like that," Paige laughed. "Instead of being cooped up in my little yard, barking at my neighbor's little dog."

"I think he'd be happy living in a car as long as he was with you," Jay added as he threw the stick back across the yard.

"He seems to like you too," she smiled as she took her turn.

"Naw, he's just happy."

Paige stood and watched Jay as he threw the stick for Harry. This seemed to be such a natural thing for the three of them to be out here, acting this way. She shook her head. *"You're just lonely, Paige. Stop this,"* she told herself as she took her turn at fetch.

"Hey, Paige, look," Jay said as he pointed to the house. Sarah was standing at the window, watching them.

"I don't believe it," Paige smiled and waved. Sarah did not wave back but continued to watch. "I think she is enjoying watching Harry run about. That gives me hope."

"It should," Jay smiled at her, genuinely happy to see her smile back.

# Chapter 9

The man smiled quietly at what had been accomplished so far. He had successfully captured her, used her, and set her free without anyone knowing, remembering, seeing. It had been over a year and there had been no repercussions. He could still watch her daily while she was unaware. She was his prize, his biggest accomplishment. "Beautiful Paige. My little pigeon. Forgetting her past and living her life as if nothing happened. If only she knew!" he smiled even brighter, remembering his time with her. He was very pleased she didn't remember. His plan had been wonderfully laid out and thus far executed.

He glanced at the old mattress in the corner and laughed at the bloodstains that covered it. "The training arena," he hissed as he ran his hand along the mattress. He then walked around the dark room, running his hand over the chair that still had the ropes attached and paused to stroke the roughness of the ropes. He glanced up at the boarded window and admired the view. Dark and damp, the way he loved it. "It's amazing what can be accomplished in a dark room," he laughed wickedly.

## Afterthoughts

He stood in the middle of the room, remembering her; seeing her hair matted and damp. He longed to see her suffer and was proud that she was going to pay.

"It's time for me to go. I must see her again!" he sneered as he eagerly left the room, closing the door quickly behind him.

# Chapter 10

The day of Richie's funeral was bright, warm, and sunny. After the previous night's storm, it felt as if it were spring instead of early September.

Paige and Aileen helped Sarah dress and fix her hair before walking her down for breakfast. Sarah was more responsive today, although she still didn't talk more than she had to and she ate only a small bite of the bacon and eggs Aileen had prepared. Paige wondered what she would be like after the funeral. Would she be able to recover? Would she be able to carry on with some semblance of a normal life? Paige couldn't imagine losing a husband and a son the way Sarah had. Even though she came close a couple of times, Paige never married. Her job was her marriage.

She didn't have time to maintain anything that important. Plus, she liked having her way and doing what she wanted without having anyone else to worry about, except for Harry, of course. He was the only outside responsibility she wanted. But she was still lonely. She still longed for a touch, a whisper, an understanding glance shared between two like individuals.

Harry crawled under the table and laid his head on Sarah's knee.

Paige watched as Sarah slowly reached down and scratched his ears.

*"What a great dog,"* she thought. It gave her hope that Sarah could recover. Maybe she should get Sarah a dog after all of this was over.

She remembered how much Harry helped. *"There's something about those loving eyes looking up at you, needing your love and attention, loving you in return,"* she thought to herself as she bit into some bacon.

The funeral service was beautiful although Paige didn't notice any of it. She didn't feel well at all. She kept fidgeting around on the pew, watching Sarah, looking at the rest of the solemn crowd. It was the same crowd that was in the same place not so long ago for Anthony's funeral plus all of Richie's friends. Paige wondered if any of them could have had a hand in Richie's death.

Sarah finally became hysterical. Paige tried to comfort her but at the same time was relieved to have some sort of emotion from her.

It helped Paige realize that Sarah was coming out of her shell and opening up to what was happening. That would help her cope. Paige held her in her arms and rocked her back and forth through the service.

She stroked her hair and held her hand while trying not to listen to the service and trying to be strong for Sarah.

Paige was thankful that the service was not a long one and the graveside service was to be even shorter. She hoped that having all of Sarah's friends around her at Aileen's during the evening that would follow would help as well. Maybe that would force Sarah to break down some of the walls she had built around herself the last couple of days.

After the graveside service was over, Aileen, Paige, and Sarah walked back to the car. Paige walked over to stand by Sarah on the sidewalk and Aileen leaned into the car to get her jacket from the back seat. A sudden prick of fear consumed Paige as she heard the squeal of tires and horrible thud. Her heart pounded as she wheeled around to find a TARC bus, Louisville's public transportation, stopped with Sarah lying on the pavement in front of it. "Oh, God!" Paige screamed as she and Aileen rushed to her. She was bleeding badly from her mouth and nose. Aileen tried to lift her, but Paige made her stop.

"Don't move her! I'll call for help!" She knelt beside Sarah and found a faint pulse. Paige grabbed her cell phone and called the police station. "An ambulance is on the way."

"She's alive." Tears streaked down Paige's cheeks as she held Sarah's hand. "She'll be okay. She has to be!" She laid her head on Sarah's shoulder.

"Okay Sarah, hang in there. Help is on the way. Please, Sarah. We need you. I need you!"

Aileen looked up at the bus driver. "What happened?" Aileen pleaded.

The bus driver stood over them, pacing back and forth, rubbing his balding head and tears streaming down his cheeks.

"I don't know..." Paige answered for him. "I stood beside her and looked your way... Before I knew it, I heard the crash. I don't know what happened. I didn't even know she moved!" She looked at the driver again. "Did she step out in front of you?"

"I'm not sure. It happened so fast. She just appeared in front of me!"

He continued to pace back and forth. "I'm so sorry. I didn't see her until it was too late. Oh, what have I done?

Why didn't I see her?" A crowd of people from the bus formed a circle around them.

"It's not your fault," Paige tried to comfort him. "It happened so fast."

Paige held Sarah's hand until the ambulance arrived. Jay came as soon as he heard Paige's call and pulled Paige away from the scene.

"Let them do their work. She'll be okay." He rocked her back and forth and brushed her hair. "She'll be okay," he repeated over and over again as Paige cried on his shoulder.

"I couldn't stop it. I should have held on to her!"

"Paige, it's not your fault. Don't blame yourself. You don't know what happened." He held her tightly and continued to try to comfort her. He held out his hand to Aileen, who seemed to be in shock. He pulled her into his arms as well and the three of them stood in silence as they watched them load Sarah into the ambulance.

"I'm going with her," Paige insisted and tried desperately to push away from Jay.

Jay grabbed her by the arm. "Come on," he said, "I'll take you both to the hospital." He led them to Aileen's car with Paige resisting all along the way. He took Aileen's arm as well. Aileen then asked Jay to call Jones on his cell phone. They followed the ambulance to the hospital and hurried to the desk as the EMT's rushed Sarah in.

After Aileen had given the nurse information about Sarah's history and insurance, she began to pace back and forth across the waiting room.

There was a long silence between the three of them as they listened to all of the hospital's intercom pages.

Aileen's husband, Jones, ran in through the door. "I came as fast as I could." Jones had already left the funeral and was halfway home when the accident happened. He quickly took Aileen into his arms. "For

Christ's sake, is she all right?"

"I don't know. We haven't heard anything yet," Aileen cried as she broke down into sobs that covered Jones's shoulder. Paige's tears started to fall rapidly as Jay put his arm tightly around her. He pulled out his handkerchief, but Paige declined taking it. Silence again took over the room.

Paige glanced around the hospital, feeling like she would explode any minute. She watched as one by one, patients were called back to be seen by the doctors. One with what looked like a broken arm, another was bundled up so much that Paige knew it must have been a fever, and yet another with his hand wrapped in a blood stained towel. As she looked toward the glass doors, she saw someone watching her from the sidewalk. She jumped up and ran to the door, with Jay running behind her.

As she ran through them, she frantically looked all around. There was no one in sight other than an elderly man pushing his wife in a wheel chair through the door.

"What is it, Paige?" Jay asked her. "Are you okay?"

"Yeah, but there was someone out here, watching me. I saw him the other day at my house in my yard. At least it looks like the same person to me."

Jay looked around and asked the old man if he had seen anyone.

The old man just shook his head and continued to push his wife into the emergency room.

"Looks like he's gone now," he added as he took Paige by the arm and led her toward the door. "Let's go back inside with Aileen."

After thirty minutes had passed, the tall, thin doctor walked in solemnly and asked everyone to join him in the chapel just off of the waiting room. "I'm so sorry," he said as he took Paige's hand. "We did all we could, but Sarah lost a lot of blood internally," he said as he placed his other hand on Aileen's arm. "She was just too weak to fight."

"No!" Paige had screamed before she realized anything had sprung from her vocal cords. Jay held her tightly to keep her from jumping up from the chair. Aileen broke down hysterically with Jones' arms wrapped tightly around her, trying to comfort her.

"What else? What else could happen?" Paige was becoming hysterical herself. "Not Sarah ... Not Sarah too! Why couldn't I stop it? *Why*?"

"Paige ... look at me ... *look at me*!" Jay grabbed Paige's shoulders and turned her to face him. "Paige, there was nothing you could have done! It's not your fault!"

"I should have stopped her ... I should have ..." Paige's sobs were becoming inaudible as she fell into Jay's arms. He held her tightly as Aileen walked over and put her arms around Paige as well.

"It's not your fault Paige. There's nothing you could have done."

Aileen tried to comfort her.

"I'm so sorry I failed her, Aileen. I've really failed her."

"No ... Paige." Aileen tried to comfort her as difficult as it was. The four of them stood sobbing in the chapel. Both Jones and Jay realized that the best they could do was to just hold them and let them fall apart.

# Chapter 11

Sarah's funeral seemed to drain most of what energy the two of them had left. Paige had a more difficult time letting go. Aileen seemed to have a harder time. The ceremony had been a long one. It seemed as if everyone wanted to say something about Sarah. There appeared to be an unusually large crowd this time and Paige wondered if some people came just out of curiosity. The graveside service was beautiful. "All three Steckler's are at rest with each other," the minister murmured and with great hope. "All of their suffering is done. They are all together in peace."

*"This is unbearable,"* Paige thought to herself. She knelt down by the casket, a long stem red rose in her hand and wept silently as her heart seemed to disappear from within her chest. She felt empty. She felt as if all of her being was being lowered into the third grave along with Sarah and she wasn't sure how to handle that. She had failed. Her best friend and sister was now gone because she had failed. The pain of that reality was unbearable. Paige wanted to crawl down into the gravesite and be buried with Sarah. That was what she

deserved.

A soft rain began to fall. Paige didn't notice at first. When she did, she lifted her head to the sky and let it wash her face. *"Wipe away my tears,"* she thought. *"I need help."* She stood up and placed the rose on Sarah's casket, gathering new strength with that simple gesture.

"I won't give up, Sarah. I will find out who destroyed your family. I give you my promise." She kissed the mahogany, laid her hand on the side, and turned to walk away. Jay and David stood side-by-side watching her. David walked to her and placed his arm around her shoulders to walk her to the car. Jay only watched from a distance, wishing he could be the one to comfort her right now.

Paige spent the next two weeks helping Aileen deal with all of the arrangements and the settlement of the Steckler's Estate. The entire estate, with the exception of the house in Gellendale Estates, was to be auctioned off with the proceeds going to The Tree House, an orphanage where Sarah had been volunteering over the last six years.

The house was to go to Richie or to the next remaining family member.

That, of course, was Paige.

On more than one occasion, while cleaning out the belongings from the house, Paige became ill. At one point, Aileen thought of taking her to the hospital but Paige resisted. David had been a tremendous help to Paige and Aileen, taking care of business whenever they became too emotional to handle it. He offered support whenever Paige felt vulnerable and gave her space when she demanded it, which was quite often.

Ian Messing, the director of the orphanage, had stopped by on several occasions to see what he could do to 'help.' He was a mousy man, with thinning gray hair and deep, stormy, gray eyes. He always seemed to wear clothing to match them. Paige was always a little nervous around him because his personality didn't match his appearance. He was strict and demanding with the orphans at The Tree House and this personality was spilling over to the handling of the Estate. Paige's lawyer, Timothy Roman had to step in and put him in his place on a regular basis. Ian was a very suspicious person and it seemed that even though all of the proceeds were going to be given to the orphanage.

Ian would not believe it unless he saw it with his own two eyes. Paige considered a restraining order against him so he would leave them alone. She figured he probably would not abide by it and it would give Paige great pleasure to arrest him.

Jay stopped by to find Ian rummaging through the garage. "Just what are you doing in here?" Jay inquired as he walked up behind Mr. Messing.

Being caught off guard, Ian quickly responded, "Just checking to see if there is anything here I want to personally bid on in next week's auction." Ian rubbed his hands together as if to hide the fact that they were shaking.

"I think you should wait and go through that when either Paige or Aileen are here with you. Or, hell man, wait for the auction! Come inside with me," Jay demanded as he prodded Ian along in the house like 'shooing' a cat away from the dinner plate. As they entered the kitchen, they found Paige and Aileen going through the silver and chatting about what to do with the house after the auction.

"Paige, can I see you for a moment?" Jay asked her, leading her away from the kitchen and leaving Ian with Aileen.

"Sure thing, partner!" she beamed at him. By the distressed look on Ian's face, she could tell that Jay just ruined Ian's day.

They walked out onto the deck at the back of the house. "How's Aileen holding up?" Jay asked her.

"She's okay. Staying busy helps, although it's unbearable going through Sarah's things. There are just too many memories." Paige let out a huge sigh and fought back the tears that were beginning to swell.

"I can't imagine." Jay put his arm around her. "How are you feeling?

Aileen told me you've been pretty ill."

"I'm fine. I'm able to keep food down now. I'm a tough cookie. You don't need to worry about me. I'll be as fit as a fiddle and back to work after this auction is over; just wait and see. Then I can get to the bottom of what happened. I have to do that for Sarah. I made her a promise."

Paige said matter-of-factly and walked to the end of the patio to look over the rail. Rage was beginning to overtake the sorrow.

"That's part of why I came by today. The investigation into the Steckler's murder case is closed. The Chief believes Richie killed Anthony, then committed suicide and that witnesses from the funeral service said Sarah stepped out in front of the bus on her own, probably because she couldn't handle it anymore."

Paige felt like she had been slapped in the face. She was silent for a moment. "They're wrong. Something else happened. Someone else was involved and I am determined to find out who it was! I can't let Sarah down. I have to close this for her!" Paige's blue eyes swelled up with tears again and Jay handed her his handkerchief.

"Let it go, Paige," Jay pleaded with her. "At least for now. It's not helping you to keep this up. You really need to let it go."

"You're wrong!" Paige's voice was getting louder. She spun around to see Ian staring at her from the window. "Get that man out of here before I throw him out myself!"

Jay left her and went into the house to talk with Ian. Paige sat down at the patio table, looking at the handkerchief. "Jay is wrong. There's someone behind this," she told herself. "There has to be and I'll find out who! I promise you, Sarah." Paige looked up as if Sarah was watching her from above, tears streaming down her face. She wiped them with the handkerchief. "God, does anyone else besides Jay still carry these things?" But today, she was glad he did.

Looking around the beautiful patio, she remembered sitting out here, cooking steaks with Anthony and Sarah, and watching Richie play with the neighbor's puppies. What a perfect, strong family they appeared to be. Everyone seemed happy and the house was full of love. *"Who would want to hurt these people?"* she asked herself. She looked around to admire the rose bushes and Crepe Myrtle trees that lined the entire patio and out to weeping willows along the creek side just beyond the yard. She was sad to think that winter was creeping in and everything would look as dead as she felt. She could see Richie's old swing set in the backyard and wondered what happened to him.

*"Why did he get so messed up in drugs? Maybe he was in trouble. Could the Steckler's have been murdered for drug money?"* Paige was more determined than ever to find out.

She lay her head on the table and shut her eyes. Visions of Richie swinging on his swing set quickly changed into visions of him swinging in the garage. She could see the ladder on the garage floor as she remembered the smell of the urine that lay in a puddle around it. She could feel the rope in her hands; the rope was in her hands …

She fell asleep.

# Chapter 12

The rope around her was tighter than she remembered. It cut into the flesh of her wrists and she could smell the stale blood around her. The lightning flashed through the window again as fear crept over her.

She could hear him coming. Paige became ill at the thought of him entering the room. She vomited violently as he opened the door.

"Come now my little pigeon. Don't be like that!" his cold voice whispered behind her. She could feel him try to clean her up. He touched her hair as she attempted to scream. Nothing would come out. She could feel herself be taken over, told to relax. She tried to see his face, but the room was too dark. *"Relax"* she kept hearing over and over again. *"Everything is fine. Just relax. Let it go."*

"Paige?" Jay's soft voice woke her. She sat up with a jolt. Trembling, she immediately became ill and raced to the rail to vomit over the side.

Jay came up behind her and held her head, as she was wretched. When she finished, he turned her around and rubbed her shoulder. "Are you okay now?" he asked her.

"I think so," she sniffed, still trembling from her dream. She was determined not to tell Jay about it. He was worried enough about her.

Did she remember the months she had been missing or was all of the stress bringing this out in her? She couldn't think about that now. "I need some water."

Jay helped her into the kitchen and poured her a glass. Aileen came in with a cold washcloth and handed it to her.

"I'll wash this thing before I give it back to you," she smiled at Jay as she wadded up his handkerchief.

"Please do! I sure don't want your cooties," he laughed at her making Paige smile.

"Feeling better?" Aileen asked her. Paige could only nod and sit down at the breakfast table, rubbing the cold cloth across her face.

Jay sat next to her. "Why don't I take you home so you can get some rest?" he begged her.

"No, I'm fine. Is Ian gone?"

"Yes," Aileen broke in. "I sent him back to the orphanage." She smacked her hands together as if to say good riddance.

"Good. I feel better without that snake around here. I don't see how Sarah put up with him. He needs to be removed from the orphanage."

Paige stood up denying Jay's arm as he offered it to her.

"I am taking you home. You need some rest," Jay demanded. After seeing Aileen's pleading look, Paige agreed.

Jay led her out to his car and helped her in. "I'm okay, Jay. Really," she told him.

"So humor me then," he smiled at her.

They rode in silence to Paige's house. Jay came in with her to make sure she made it in okay. "Take a shower and get ready for bed. I'll see if I can find some crackers and ginger ale or something." He patted her shoulder as he pushed her in the direction of her bathroom.

Paige didn't argue. Any other time she would have but it was nice to not be alone. As she showered, Paige let the hot water run over her, relieving her tense muscles. She enjoyed the vanilla scent of her shampoo and shower gels and let these things relax her. She was calm now. Everything was going to be fine. She knew this somehow.

Everything was set back to right again in her mind. *"Relax. Be calm, still. No ... fight this feeling!"* she told herself. *"Nothing is right. Nothing is fine. What is going on with me?"* She felt the tears well up in her eyes.

*"Am I going crazy?"* She shook her head trying to clear her thoughts and convince herself that she needed rest. Tomorrow she could think clearly again. Rest would clear her head of the images of the past she wanted to forget. Instead, the fear of dreaming and remembering them crept back into her mind. *"At this point, I'm not sure what I need,"* she thought to herself.

Paige turned the water off and reached for her towel. She dried off and wrapped the towel around her, then looked in the mirror. The dark circles under her eyes made her cringe. She was losing weight rapidly through all of this and she really didn't have any to lose. *"I look like a bloody skeleton,"* she thought. She picked up her silver-handled brush and ran it through her long brown hair. *"Even my hair is falling out!"* she thought as she cleaned out the brush and threw the hair in the trashcan. She brushed her teeth quickly and walked out of the bathroom, still wrapped in the towel.

"Nice legs!" Jay laughed from the kitchen as he saw Paige emerge from the bathroom.

"I forgot you were here," she blushed as she pulled the towel tighter around her. "I'll be right back." She hurried down the hall and put on her silk pajamas. Embarrassed, she walked back to the kitchen.

"I'm sorry!" she smiled.

"Don't be! Those were the nicest set of legs I've seen in a long time!"

"Better not let Dolly hear you say that!" Paige laughed.

"Well, she's not exactly in the picture anymore." Jay shrugged and played with a spoon that was lying on the counter.

Paige suddenly realized how out of touch she was with him since Sarah died. "I'm sorry. I didn't know. What happened?" She walked over and stood beside him.

"That's okay. I didn't tell you," he forced a tiny smile. "Things just didn't work out for us. She's now seeing Phil Meeks. Remember him?"

He laughed thinking about how he had been dumped for the pudgy Phil. "How are things with David?"

"Fine. He's been great. He's actually helped Aileen a lot lately. He is gone to Las Vegas for a book signing there and should be back next week." Paige felt guilty talking about David to Jay. She hoped it wasn't bothering him to hear that her relationship was doing well while his had fallen apart.

He handed her a lime soda he found in the fridge. She smiled and took the can from him. As she took a drink and sat the can on the kitchen table, Jay took her into his arms for a moment. "I'm so sorry you've had to go through this," he whispered in her ear. She let her arms go around his waist. She needed to be held. Jay rubbed her back as he held her. He enjoyed her damp, vanilla scented hair against his face as he fought off the urge to kiss her. He was startled at the thought. He hadn't felt that way about her before. Could she feel his heart start to pound in his chest? He could feel her relax in his arms as he realized he didn't want to leave her. He wanted to be here with her, to comfort her, to wipe away her tears. He held her tight and kissed her hair. He felt her hold onto him tighter and heard her sigh as she rested her head on his shoulder. She needed him to be there. He knew it.

Paige felt so comfortable in his arms. This was the safest she had felt in quite some time. She had tried to be so independent through all of this. It was nice to let him hold her up and comfort her even though she had a hard time admitting that to herself and knew she would never admit that to him out loud. Even Harry seemed to approve. He didn't try to squeeze his way in between them as he always did with David.

Jay finally let her go and she sat down at the table to drink her soda and nibble on the saltines he had found for her.

"I guess I need to eat. I happened to stop and look at myself in the mirror today and I look horrid!" she tried to force a smile.

"You're always beautiful." Jay patted her hand.

"By whose standards?" she laughed.

"By anyone who has eyes," he smiled at her. When she smiled back warmly, his heart leaped in his chest. Their eyes maintained contact for a few seconds that felt like a lifetime for Jay.

"Paige," he said as he gently took her hand. "You and I have been partners and friends for years. I feel like I've known you my entire life," he took a deep breath and continued. "What I'm

trying to say here is that I really care about you and I am here if you need me. However, it is that you may need me."

Squeezing his hand, she replied, "I know that and I feel the same way. I'm all right, Jay. I promise." Paige looked away trying to hide the lie she just told him.

"I know you're strong, Paige. But sometimes you have to let someone help you. There's nothing wrong with leaning on someone. You don't have to bear everything alone."

She only smiled slightly keeping her eyes away from his gaze.

# Chapter 13

Paige woke up the next morning feeling like a new person. She slept the entire night without dreaming, at least any that she could remember.

Jay had stayed over and slept on the couch. She liked knowing that he was so close by if she needed him. Part of her had wished that he had come to bed with her so he could hold her and let her sleep.

Jay, on the other hand, didn't sleep well at all. He struggled all night with the thought of her in the other room. He wanted to be with her, but he knew that would be the wrong thing to do. He even got off the couch several times and paced around the living room before heading toward her room at least three times, just to turn around and go sit back down. *"She is my partner. She has David. She doesn't feel the same,"* he kept telling himself over and over again not wanting her to think that he was taking advantage of her while she was vulnerable. "You're driving yourself crazy!" he chuckled to himself lightly, tossing around on the couch.

"Why's that?" Paige asked from the corner of the room. Startled, Jay sat straight up.

"Nothing. Just talking to myself," he tried to recover. "How are you feeling?"

"Much better. Thank you so much for staying. I slept like a baby."

She stretched her long arms over her head. Harry ran to greet her.

After hugging and scratching him, she opened the door and let him out.

"I'm glad you let me help." He stood and walked over to her and gave her a hug. Paige kissed him on the cheek making Jay tremble. His hand brushed across her cheek as he looked at her.

"You've been such a great friend," she smiled warmly at him. Jay's mouth was dry at the thought of kissing her. It would be easy to right now as he rubbed his thumb along her jaw line. The telephone ringing as Paige walked away to answer it interrupted his thought.

"Hey, David!" she beamed as Jay's heart dropped into his feet. "Did you win big at the tables? … Yeah … No kidding? … Wow, you'd better bring back something nice for me then … She's fine … she's busy getting ready for the auction. I think that's what is keeping her sane right now…I'm okay…" Jay's heart dropped again as he became afraid that Paige was about to tell David he had stayed the night. "I slept really well last night so I feel much better today … When will you be back? … Great … see you then … Bye now." Paige hung up the phone and looked at Jay. He was staring out the picture window at the bird feeder. She walked over and placed her hand on his shoulder.

He automatically put his hand over hers. "Come on, let's go get some breakfast. Do you feel like eating?" he asked.

"I'm famished!" she beamed at him.

They dressed quickly and headed out for Pauline's Café at the end of Paige's street. Paige ordered scrambled eggs, toast, and bacon while Jay only ordered oatmeal. He watched her as she devoured her meal and thought how great it was to see her feeling better and hoped had he played a small part in making that happen. Admiring the simple, yet alluring features of her face and how she always wore her hair casually about her shoulders. *"I'd bet she'd look great in a baseball cap,"* he mused.

He realized he needed to be here for her but to not let himself get too close. This was a task that he didn't know how he was going to balance knowing he had to work with her every day and wanting to be there for whatever, whenever she needed him. Besides Aileen and David, she really didn't have anyone anymore. His heart broke for her and he felt like his head was spinning in circles.

He looked around the cafe to try to take his mind off of things.

The cafe was noisy and crowded. The smell of bacon and waffles filled the room with such wonderful fragrances that should have made him hungry. Somehow, it didn't. He watched an elderly couple. They looked so pleasant. The man was cutting his wife's ham into pieces to make it easier for her and then helped her to use her fork to eat the pieces.

There was such love in his eyes as he helped her. Jay was sure the wife had probably had a stroke and was struggling to learn things all over again. He wondered if this was a permanent situation. *"Would the old man get tired of helping her? What would happen if he passed on before her or ended up in the same state?"* Yet, there he was taking care of her. The years of love they'd naturally shared made Jay extremely jealous. Would he find that someday? As he glanced at Paige, he hoped she would find that as well.

*"Okay, that's not working,"* he thought to himself as

he looked away, noticing Paige watching him intently.

"What's going on in that incredibly busy mind there?" she asked him, trying to look cute.

He played with the corner of his napkin. "Just watching the elderly couple over there. He is really taking care of her isn't he?"

"Yeah, it's really sweet," she sighed. "They give me hope. Ah well, maybe someday I'll have that."

"You don't think you and David will get there?" he asked hopefully.

"I don't know. I can't tell if he's the right one. Maybe I'll never find the right one." She shrugged her shoulders and sighed.

Jay's heart skipped a beat.

"It started out so perfect, David and me. We seemed to have so much in common and he appeared to be so totally in love with me.

Now …" she blushed looking at him. "You don't want to hear that."

"Sure I do. I'm your partner as well as your friend," Jay smiled and winked at her.

"Okay, you asked for it." She toyed with the corner of her napkin just as Jay had done. "Even before Anthony's death he was becoming more distant. When he was around it felt like he was a million miles away. I didn't know how to handle that. I tried to figure out if I had done something wrong or if he was just dealing with something. I even wondered if he had changed his mind about us. After all, I wasn't around much myself with work and all."

"Don't blame yourself, Paige. Things happen for a reason."

"I know, I know. I think the only reason he comes around now is because with all I've been going through he hasn't had the heart to tell me anything else." She took a drink of her coffee.

"Then again, maybe all of this made him realize that he wants to be around," Jay choked on the words, knowing that was what happened to him.

"I don't know. Maybe after things settle down, he and I can have a long heart to heart and get to the bottom of some things."

"That sounds like a good idea. I don't think Dolly and I were ever on the same page. She always seemed to want something different," he laughed. "I hope pudgy Phil has better luck than I did."

Paige had to laugh at that. She couldn't imagine why anyone would turn away from Jay and toward Phil, except for the fact that Phil had a lot of money.

It was nice to sit and talk to Jay. She felt their bond of friendship growing stronger. Paige really needed that, realizing that he and Aileen were all she had. She was beginning to wonder if, in the end, David was going to be there for her at all. The thought saddened her, but it didn't break her heart.

Paige started feeling sorry for herself again. Self-pity was not a luxury she was going to allow herself have. She needed to pull herself together and concentrate on finding out what actually happened to the Stecklers. To prove how strong she was, she paid the bill for breakfast despite the opposition from Jay. He shook his head at her but decided it was best to let her win this battle.

After Jay had dropped Paige off at her house, she decided to write in her journal. It would be nice to write down a few good things for a change.

> *"Jay and I are becoming closer as friends, which is something I have in short supply now. It's nice to know that he is here and that he cares for me. I'm not quite sure how I feel about it, though.*

*Only time will tell, but it's nice to write something positive."*

Paige sighed, closed the journal, and hugged it. It did feel good to write something positive and what she perceived to be sane. Hoping that she was on the way to recovery, she put the journal on her nightstand and went to take a bath.

# Chapter 14

The man was becoming impatient. For the first time, he felt like he was losing control. His grip on everyone was quickly sliding away.

He slowly smiled again as he walked toward the door. He turned once more to look at the room. Confidence and pride began to swell in him as he remembered all that he had accomplished already. He took pride in all of the pain he caused her to make her weak. He knew that he could once again regain complete control. It was not going to fall apart now. Not ever.

# Chapter 15

Jay tried to avoid getting too close to Paige without letting her know.

He wanted to still be there whenever she needed him, but he would not allow himself to get too emotionally attached. He knew he had fallen in love with Paige over the last month, yet still didn't know how he was going to handle it. For now, he decided, avoidance was best. He would have to get over it and find someone new. It was damn hard to be near her, wanting her, and not being able to have her. He realized he was making himself miserable whenever she would smile at him or casually touch his arm as they worked together at the auction. He had to keep himself from yelling at her to get her away from him but at the same time he didn't want her to be away from him at all. He felt like a dog chasing his tail in a chase he'll never win and if he did, it would hurt terribly.

Paige was feeling his distance. Here again, she was pushing someone away from her. First David, now Jay, and she wondered what might happen next. *"At least I still have Harry,"* she thought to herself as she dried off from her morning shower. When she looked into the mirror, she realized she looked healthier. Some of the color had returned to her face and her eyes did not look as dark and sunken as they had been. She smiled at her reflection and got ready for the day.

The auction was now over and hopefully, Ian was happy with all of the proceeds. The Tree House was now over two million dollars richer.

This meant that Paige was going back to work.

Jay paced around his office. He was doing this a lot more often lately but today, he was really nervous. He'd have to face Paige on a daily basis and hoped things would get back to normal as they would fight over cases and wear on each other's nerves. That would help him get over her. He pictured her stubbornly arguing her point as if hers was the only one that mattered. Smiling he tried to remember all of the picky little things she used to do to aggravate him and to get his blood boiling; things he now thought were cute.

"God I've got it bad," he said to himself as he paced around his office, picking up his baseball bat and rolling it in his hands. "Maybe I should knock some sense into myself. Yeah, that'll work." He held the bat up high and lowered it laughing.

Paige was nervous as well. It had been nearly two months since she had worked full time. She knew she had her work cut out for her in finding who murdered Anthony Steckler and why Richie had killed himself. She didn't care if the case was officially closed. It wasn't closed for Paige. She had a promise to keep.

As she walked into the police station, the newest rookie, Hannah, met her at the door and introduced herself. She handed Paige a pink envelope that was delivered to the station late last week. It was hand written with only her name. The handwriting was elegant and the back seal was marked Confidential.

Paige pondered this for a moment, running her fingers over the seal before walking into Jay's office.

"Hey there! Welcome back!" Jay tried to sound cheerful and was overdoing the tone. He laid the baseball bat back down on the desk.

"It's good to be back!" she smiled. "What's the scoop? Where are the Steckler files?"

Jay only smiled at her. "Under S," he laughed.

"Okay, smart ass. I see you haven't missed a beat. You're not planning on using that thing are you?" she laughed and pointed at the bat. She whirled around and walked out of the office and headed for the filing cabinet. Speechless, Jay stood motionless as he watched her walk away.

With shaking hands, Paige flipped through the cabinet and pulled the file. She hugged it to her chest and walked to her office. She laid the pink envelope aside and opened the Steckler file. She read each page carefully, studying for any mistake, looking for any missed lead. Nausea crept over her as she examined the pictures of the crime scenes so she decided to grab a cup of coffee. She walked past Jay's office toward the break room. When she entered the room, she was greeted with several "Welcome backs" and "We missed yous". This made her feel a little better. She worked her way to the coffee pot. As she filled the cup with cream and sugar, she pictured Anthony, lying on the bedroom floor, his face blue and swollen. She tried to remember everything about the crime scene. Everything in the room looked normal. Other than the body on the floor, there was no sign of a struggle. Remembering the pictures of Anthony that showed all of the bruising around his neck, she could feel her hands around his neck, squeezing tighter and tighter until he fell to the floor. Suddenly the coffee cup slipped from her hand and shattered on the break room floor. Paige grabbed the countertop and tried to steady herself.

"Here, I'll get that!" Jay, who had walked in behind Paige, started cleaning up the mess. Paige stood there shaking. "You okay?" he asked as he looked up at her while wiping up the coffee.

"Yeah, just need that first cup of Joe," she tried to smile but Jay could see through her facade and knew something was wrong.

"You go sit. I'll clean this up and bring ya a fresh cup with tons of cream and sugar," he added with a wink. Paige didn't argue and walked back to her office, still shaking and trying to figure out what she had just seen.

As she sat at the desk, she saw the envelope. She took a deep breath, slid her finger under the seal and opened the letter. Inside was a single piece of rose-colored paper that opened to reveal the same neat handwriting. *"Whoever wrote this, really took their time,"* she thought to herself as she began to read.

*Dear Paige Aldridge,*

*I am writing to you because I know what you have been going through. I know about your memories of the dark room. If you want some answers, please think of me when you are alone and I will be there.*

*Junna Breck*

*"What the hell is this about?"* she asked herself as she saw Jay coming her way. Hurriedly, she stuffed the paper in her desk drawer. She wasn't ready to discuss this with anyone.

"Here you go," Jay smiled and handed her the coffee. She tried to return the smile as she took it from him, but her hands were still shaking.

"Thanks a bunch. Do you have any leads that aren't in the files?"

She tried to divert his attention away from her hands and the fact that her drawer was partly open with the pink paper sticking out.

"No. That's the problem, there is nothing but what the chief feels is the obvious," he sighed and sat down in the chair across from her desk.

He was worried about her, as she looked very pale and sick again and fought back the urge to hug her.

"You don't feel that way?" she asked hopefully, as she leaned toward her desk to push the drawer closed further.

"I've not always gone with you on your hunches, partner, and I don't want to give you any false hopes. It is just too obvious." He took a long drink of his own coffee and brushed the hair out of his face. His hair had grown out a lot lately, she noticed. It looked great on him.

"I just feel there is something else going on. Someone else involved," she said. As she very carefully placed the coffee cup on her desk, she thought about the letter.

Jay stood and started to leave but turned around to look at Paige. He half opened his mouth to speak, then turned back around and walked out. Paige was looking at her desk drawer, waiting for him to get back to his office. She opened the drawer and re-read the letter. *"Think of me when you are alone and I will be there,"* she repeated over and over.

He placed the letter back in the drawer and looked at the file again.

*"There has to be something, some small clue that*

*we've overlooked."* She thought about the vision she had in the break room. *"Why can I feel my hands around his neck? Why did I feel the rope in my hands when I thought about Richie? Am I thinking too hard about it all? Is everything getting under my skin too much, making me imagine these things? And who the heck is Junna Breck and what does she have to do with me? Why do I remember that dark room, and who is that man?"*

Paige's eyes began to fill with tears as she stood and hastily ran to the bathroom. After making sure no one else was in there, she sat down, quickly grabbed some toilet paper and wept. She cried harder than she had ever cried. It seemed to her that she cried for a half an hour and wondered if anyone could hear her sobs from outside. Her head was whirling and she was beginning to feel ill again. Taking a deep breath, she leaned her head back to try to stop the tears. She felt a sense of calm envelop her and she could hear a voice, *"You're okay. Calm down. Breathe. Everything is fine. Just breathe."*

After a few moments, she walked out of the stall and to the sink.

"So much for make-up," she sighed as she regretted actually putting some on. She decided to splash cold water on her face to bring down the swelling around her eyes. When Paige felt she was as presentable as she was going to get, she held up her head, squared her shoulders, and walked back to her office.

# Chapter 16

After her first day back to work, Paige was exhausted. Deciding to take the Steckler file and the letter home with her and think about what to do next, she packed her bag and reached for what was left of a soft drink she had purchased at lunch, knocking it over. "Damn, you are clumsy!" said a deep voice from the doorway.

"David!" Paige ran over and gave him a hug. "I was beginning to wonder if you would be here today!"

"Just got in," he said as he kissed her. "How are you holding up?"

"I'm fine. Great now that you are here," she hugged him tightly and kissed him again.

From the door of his office, Jay watched David and Paige. He rubbed his eyes with both of his hands thinking how stupid he was to even think about her. She was obviously happy with David after all. He turned around and went back in his office to grab his keys and head out of the door. Paige saw him pass and could tell that something was wrong. She tried to walk to him, but David stopped her. "What do you want for dinner? Just name it and it's yours!" He was beaming. His dark blonde hair was messier than usual, making Paige wonder if he was using some new hair gel.

"Oh, I don't know. I've not had much of an appetite lately." She toyed with the files on her desk, trying to figure out what to take with her, slipping everything she thought she could possibly look at in her briefcase.

"You never have my dear," he smiled at her and kissed her again.

"I've missed you so much!"

"I've missed you too!" She reached up and hugged him before turning back around to pick up what she had tucked away to take home.

They walked out to David's Mercedes and drove to Hennery's, an extravagant French Restaurant in Louisville. They made small talk along the way about some of the sights David had seen and things he had done while he was away.

"David, I'm not dressed for this," Paige said as she looked down at the sweater she had on and the khaki pants with coffee stains on the leg, then remembered that she no longer had on make-up.

"Don't worry about that. No one will notice," he winked at her.

"We have so much catching up to do." He took her hand and led her through the door.

Francis, the maitre d', led them to David's usual table. After ordering the wine and dinner as usual, he then turned to look at Paige. "You haven't asked me about the book."

"So, how's the book doing?" she smiled at him as if she had come up with the question all by herself. She was beginning to see how she pushed people off. Not showing an interest, whether or not intentional, is never a good thing in a relationship. Promising herself that she needed to think of others first, she turned her attention back toward David.

"It's ten on the New York Times." His big toothy smile was too bright to overlook from across the room.

"Oh David, that's wonderful!" Paige tried not to squeal too loudly, glancing over her shoulders to make sure she hadn't caused a scene.

Paige was thankful for the dim lights as everyone looked as if they were enjoying their own meals and conversation. She felt she was safe from the scene.

"I hope to break the top five by next week." He took her hand and smiled at her.

For some reason, as Paige looked at him, she didn't feel quite right.

David didn't seem the same to her. This would have been something he would have told her in private so they could really celebrate together with several bottles of wine. She shook off the notion. It had been a couple of weeks since they actually spent time together and that was while getting ready for the auction. Paige squeezed his hand. "I have no doubt." She glanced over David's shoulder to find Ian Messing sitting with what looked to be a prostitute.

"Oh God, what is he doing here?" She turned to look at David instead.

"Who?" he asked trying not to look around.

"That idiot of a man, Ian Messing, from the orphanage. He's no doubt wasting the orphanage's money on that whore over there." She tried not to look again as the waiter poured more wine. The woman he was with had blonde hair in what appeared to be a beehive hairdo and had enough make-up on to rival Cleopatra, even in the dim light.

Paige could not help but laugh at her.

David chuckled. "Well, whatever floats his boat," he finally said as he shrugged his shoulders.

"That's just disgusting. The children need the money

more than he needs that whore. From what I understand, he's mean and hateful to the children. I doubt they see a penny of what Sarah has done for them." She rubbed her hand across her forehead.

"Being a little harsh, are we? That may be his wife." David finally turned to see the woman and laughed himself.

"Oh come on. I would even give her more credit than to marry that!" Paige found herself laughing hard for the first time in days.

The rest of dinner went pleasantly as David told her about Las Vegas and how many autographs he thought he had signed with his very cramped hands. Paige needed the chance to think about other things and to relax. It felt good to relax. Everything is falling into place, safe and secure. She allowed herself to feel that way for a while. The wine was helping, but it was also making her very sleepy. She had to fight to keep her eyes open as David rattled on and on about his new fans.

Finally, David took her back to work to get her car and kissed her goodbye at the car door. He told her he had to be on a six-thirty flight back to New York in the morning and wanted to go home and answer a few emails, and study a presentation he was giving the next day.

After giving him one long last hug, Paige opened the door of her Honda, hopped in, and started the engine. Looking back at the station, she noticed that Jay was back in his office. She shut the engine off and decided to go in and talk to him, wanting to find out what had been bothering him today. She hoped that she hadn't offended him by wanting to pour over the Steckler files and not being interested in what was going on with him.

As she climbed out of the car, she could see someone peering from around the corner. "Who are you?" she yelled at them. "Why are you following me?" She ran towards the corner and looked down the alley.

There was no one in sight. "I think I'm going crazy," she said as she placed her hand on her forehead and headed toward the door of the station.

When she walked up to his office door, she could see nothing but the back of his head as he was staring at the picture of a golf course he had hanging behind his desk. His hands were behind his head and he was obviously deep in thought about something. She noticed he had neatly arranged everything on his desk. He was always a slob; always had more important things to do than keep his office cleaned and organized, claiming he had a method to his madness that only he could understand. Paige believed him on that one.

"Dreaming of a golf vacation?" she asked him making him jump.

"No, just wishing I was somewhere else," he smiled at her as he turned around. "What are you doing back here? David just got back and I figured you two would be out on some hot date or something."

He tried to sound cheerful even though his heart was breaking.

"He has some things to take care of before he flies to New York tomorrow. Why are you here?" She walked around to the side of his desk for a better look.

"Nowhere else to be, I guess," Jay shrugged and scratched his head.

"You need to be out finding a new girlfriend. Get back in the saddle!

Hey, I know a girl," she giggled.

"Yeah, yeah, yeah. I'm a little saddle sore right now." He stood up, pretending to rub his behind.

"I'm sorry. That was really insensitive of me wasn't it?" Paige walked over and put her hand on his arm. She felt him pull away. She had never seen him like this and she was determined to figure out what was going on.

"No, it's okay. I really don't want to find someone right now. It's good to be free!" He sat back down.

"Yeah, I can tell," she said sarcastically, wanting to hug him. He had been there so much for her lately. She smiled down at him, trying to get him to smile, but he didn't budge.

"What is it, Jay?"

"Nothing, I'm fine," he said as he stood again and walked away from her. She followed.

"Come here," she cooed and pulled him to her and hugged him tightly. She could feel him loosen up and hug her back. Realizing she had made some small progress, she added, "You can talk to me you know. We're partners right?"

He fought the urge to kiss her. He wanted to feel her pressed against him and stroke her hair. But, instead, he pushed her away. "I'm okay. Really. I'm just tired and maybe feeling a little sorry for myself."

Paige could see him tense up again. She didn't stop him from grabbing her holding and her tighter. She wanted him to tell her more of what was bothering him. She wanted to be there for him even if he just needed to be held. He held on to her as if his life depended on it.

Maybe, it did, at least at that moment. He finally let her go.

"I'm serious, Jay. You've been here so much for me lately. Let me return the favor. Please. I'll just listen and not pick on you. I promise," she batted her eyelashes at him and smiled a devious little smile.

"Thanks, Paige. I know you're here for me too. I really appreciate it but I really am fine. I'm glad you are back. I've missed you," he said and softened up to hug her gently.

Paige felt like she had a small victory by helping him lighten up and hopefully, put him in a better mood. "I've missed you too. I know I've been a little difficult lately.

Hopefully, I can get everything put behind me soon and get back to being my old self."

"Don't we all?" he laughed, slapping her on the arm.

"Now that's better. I'd much rather have you telling me what's what, than moping around all the time. Besides, since when do you clean off your desk? I can actually see the wood!"

"Well, I've had a lot more time lately without you bugging me every five minutes. Now I guess it will be a mess again!" He couldn't help himself, but he couldn't keep his arms from going around again to give her a big hug and a kiss her on the cheek.

"Welcome back. I really mean it."

"Thanks. It's good to be back, but I think I'll go home now and start all over again tomorrow. I need to figure out what else I can do to bug the heck out of you."

# Chapter 17

It was late when Paige got home. She decided to go to sleep and look at the files tomorrow with fresh eyes. Her head was spinning with David's success and Jay's problems. It was good for her to think of other things for now and to begin looking at the case files again later.

She took her shower, put on the silkiest pajamas she could find and went to bed.

As she drifted softly off to sleep, she dreamt of an aquarium of bright orange goldfish. She was watching them swim peacefully through the tank. The only care they had in the world was when the food was going to be dropped into the water the next time. Their long golden fins moved gracefully through the water, pushing them along from one side of the tank to the other. Paige felt as if she floated along with them, feeling the water gently brush her skin. The dream then drifted to a beautiful waterfall that fell from a very high cliff. The water was only a small stream and fell gently on the rocks below. She could hear the sounds of the water and feel the mist on her face as a breeze gently moved the air around her. She noticed a bright rainbow extending from the base of the waterfall that seemed to reach out forever. Each color vividly displayed. Lying on the bank of the river below the waterfall, she allowed the mist to fall over her and it seemed to wash away all of her cares and fears. The bank became like a cloud as she felt as if she were drifting into the sky. Peace, such wonderful peace. Flying high above the world, all of her troubles, all of the pain, seemed so far removed from her. The warmth of the sunshine made her feel safe, secure.

The alarm clock rang intensely on her nightstand and she had to struggle to wake up. "It can't be morning already!" Paige complained as she placed her feet on the floor. The coolness of her hardwood floors helped to bring her to consciousness. Stretching her arms in the air, she stood up. She felt wonderful this morning. The stiffness in her body was gone and she was struggling against the urge to crawl back into bed and relax more. She remembered her dream and thought about how nice it was to not have nightmares. She exhaled a long breath and decided to make coffee. *"I've got a long day ahead of me,"* she thought.

After strolling into the kitchen, she grabbed the newspaper from the doorstep as Harry ran out. Her mouth dropped. On the front page was David with a longhaired blonde on his arm. They looked like they were trying to avoid having their photo taken. It reminded her of the cover of a tabloid. She could not see the woman's face in the picture as she was obviously trying to hide it under her hair and she kept her hand between the camera and her face. The caption read, "Local writer scores big." The article was about David's success with his book, *The Artic,* but it didn't mention who the woman was. Paige tried to push this out of her mind. It could have been anyone. She was proud of David and what he had finally accomplished and she was not going to mess things up with him by worrying about a picture in the paper. It could be anyone, a publicist, fan, anyone. She sat the paper down and decided to get ready to go to work.

As she walked by the kitchen table, she remembered the letter. She pulled it from her briefcase and read it once again. As she was thinking about the contents, there was a knock on her door. She peeked through the curtain to see a small, brown-haired woman standing there, wearing a short gray business suit that fit her small frame beautifully. Her hair was neat and tidy and the glasses she wore made her resemble what Paige would picture as a librarian, so she opened the door.

"Can I help you?" she asked the woman.

"I believe I'm here to help you," she said as she held out her hand. "I'm Junna Breck."

As Paige started to reach for her hand, she pulled back momentarily.

Catching her breath, she timidly shook her hand. "What is it you want to help me with?" Paige considered shutting the door in her face.

"I want to help you with your memories. I can see what you are going through," Junna didn't smile. She only stood there confidently.

"I don't understand. What is it that you think you know?" Paige asked nervously, once again wanting to shut the door in her face.

"Let me start by saying that I know you dreamt about goldfish and waterfalls last night."

Paige turned from the door and sat down quickly at the kitchen table, leaving the door open. "May I come in?" Junna asked her as she poked her head around the open door. Paige could only nod. Junna walked in and slowly sat down at the table. "I have a lot to tell you. I'm sure you won't believe me at first, but I have to try."

Paige cast a puzzled glance. "How did you know my dreams? Don't tell me you are some kind of psychic!"

She sounded agitated.

"No, I'm not a psychic. I can't see into the future, just the present, like you, only at a different level." She reached for Paige's hand and Paige quickly pulled it away.

"Relax Paige. I need you to do something first." Junna placed both of her hands flat on the table. "Please, just think outside yourself. Don't form words or pictures in your mind. Just let yourself understand what I tell you without thinking in words. Can you do that?"

"I'm not sure I understand," Paige looked at her and somehow a feeling of trust came over her.

"That's it. Just feel things. Don't think them. Some people can read the words and pictures in your mind. Feelings cannot be read at all. They can only be guessed at. Right now, I can tell you are feeling something and you just thought of how crazy you think I am."

Junna was right. Paige blushed because she was saying to herself that Junna was crazy. But then again, who wouldn't? It was an obvious guess on Junna's part. Paige rubbed her face with both hands and ran her fingers through her hair.

"Clear your mind Paige and just listen to me carefully." Junna paused for a moment, looking at Paige. "There are three levels of consciousness that all of us have. One level is the one of words and pictures in our thoughts and dreams. These are in the collective conscious. It's like a dimension for our thoughts. We all share in the collective conscious.

The second level is one of our feelings and only we can see that clearly.

Others can get a sense of it, but only we, ourselves understand it. That is like knowing something is wrong with someone, but you can't put your finger on it." Junna then touched Paige's hand again. "The third level is that of our immediate surroundings like what you see and touch. Only those around us can share in that with us. But they can't experience them like you do unless you form the words in your mind.

Am I making sense?"

"I think so." Strangely enough, she did.

"There are people that can tap into the collective conscious at will.

They can hear the thoughts as the thoughts pass through it. They are called readers. I am one of those. That's how I knew about your dreams.

You can stop me by clearing your mind and by only feeling, hearing, seeing, and touching things. Don't think about them or form words and pictures in your mind. As soon as your thoughts go through the conscious they are gone. They do not stay as if they were a permanent record of what you were thinking. Then they become part of your memory and can only be brought back by you thinking about them again. Someone has to catch them at the precise time you are thinking them. Do you understand?"

"I think so," that seemed to be the only words that Paige could form.

"I can't tell you any more now, Paige. I can help you, but I need you to learn to block me from your mind. If you can block me, you can stop anyone from reading you. I am going to leave you with this. Try to clear your mind as often as possible on things you do not want anyone else to know. Say things out loud instead of thinking them. That way, they are part of your surroundings and not in the collective conscious.

When you are ready, I will come back. It was a great pleasure meeting you." With that, Junna took her hand from Paige's and walked out the door.

# Chapter 18

Paige sat in silence for most of an hour. *"Am I dreaming?"* she thought to herself. *"Wake up, Paige. This is just a nightmare."* She finally stood up and walked to the kitchen sink and splashed cold water on her face. *"I have to be dreaming."* She dried off with a dishtowel and walked back to the table. There was the note staring back at her. She picked it up and rubbed it between her fingers. "What is this all about," she muttered aloud to herself as she sighed and placed the letter back on the table.

She decided that she was better off going to work and thinking about something else for a while. She was determined to make good on her promise to Sarah and refused to let her down again.

As she showered, she tried to clear her mind and only feel the water and smell the shampoo. She could hear Junna saying, *"Good"* as if she were in the room with her. "I am going crazy!" Paige shouted as she hit the water tap and grabbed her towel. She hurried and climbed into her clothes, dried her hair, grabbed her bag and headed out the door.

When she pulled into the station, she thought about whether or not to tell Jay about what happened this morning. Would he think she was crazy as well? She sighed and got out of the car and headed for the door. As her hand touched the door handle, she was suddenly chilled to the bone. She felt as if someone's hands were on her shoulders, trying to massage her, telling her to relax and forget what happened this morning. As she started to give into the feeling, the thought came to her to clear her mind. She shut her eyes and felt the door handle under her hand, listened to the cars buzzing down the road behind her and felt the weight of the bag on her shoulder. Paige suddenly felt better and she opened the door.

*"What in the hell was that?"* She thought to herself as she walked to her desk. Her hands were trembling uncontrollably. *"It had to be Junna. What is Junna up to? Is she getting into my mind?"* She slammed the bag on her desk and headed out for coffee looking toward Jay's office as she went. It was empty. Right now, she was glad of that. She wouldn't have to face him with the temptation to tell him everything, at least not right now. Needing to figure out what was going on in her head before she could begin to share it with anyone; she wondered if she should go back to Dr. Southerland. "Maybe this is something he can help me with," she whispered out loud, just in case.

She fixed her coffee and went back to her office to start looking at the Steckler file again. It occurred to her that Junna may be trying to help her solve the murders. Paige tried to clear her mind and looked at the pictures again. As she looked at the newspaper clipping of the scene of Sarah's death, Paige suddenly felt ill. She grabbed her coffee and took a good long drink then leaned back in her chair and shut her eyes. "Just where is this collective conscious? Where do my thoughts go?" she whispered as she tried to feel where her thoughts went. "Jay would really think I'm crazy."

As she started wondering where he was, she could hear words form in her head. *"Oh no. She's here now. Come on Jay, get a grip on yourself."*

Paige opened her eyes to see Jay walking hurriedly by her office and into his.

"Did I just hear him?" she asked herself, shaking off the crazy thought. She wondered if she should go talk to him. He didn't seem to acknowledge her as he passed. She figured he probably had a lot on his mind this morning and really wasn't avoiding her. At least she hoped not. Had she done something to him lately to upset him or make him not want to be around her? She knew something was wrong and she remembered Junna mentioning how she could feel something was wrong with someone but not know what it was. That was supposed to be another level of consciousness. She decided to go talk to him, feeling confident in knowing that something was wrong.

When she entered his office, he was opening the newspaper across his desk. "Hey partner," he shot a smile at her.

"Good morning. Did you sleep well?"

"No, but I never do. How are you?"

The conversation appeared to Paige to be going too much like they were two people that were merely acquaintances. "I slept like a baby," she responded. "Tell me, Jay, have I done something wrong? You don't seem the same to me."

"No, no. I'm just under a lot of stress I guess. I'm sorry. Have you found any missed leads?" He was changing the subject and Paige could see right through him.

"No," she lied. "Nothing new." Junna may not be a

lead and she dared not tell him anything about her. "I guess I'll get back to it."

She turned and walked back to her office wondering what it could be that she had done to make him avoid her. Had she pestered him too much to talk? Was he taking his breakup harder than he was willing to admit? Maybe he was just under too much stress, knowing she had put a lot on him lately.

Jay just sighed. He knew he wasn't handling things very well and decided to ask her to lunch later. If they were to be friends, he would have to treat her like one and stop being standoffish. He wanted to kick himself for not talking to her more and seeing how she was truly feeling. After all, he wanted to ask her if she had any more dreams.

This would all have to wait for lunch, he decided.

As he sat down at his desk, he pretended to read the newspaper.

All of his thoughts were focused on Paige. He could still feel his arms around her, the smell of her hair, and the sound of her voice. All of these things drove him crazy. So many emotions and feelings bounced around in him that his stomach felt weak and his head was spinning.

"Oh, what I wouldn't give for a drink," he whispered to himself as he lightly banged his forehead on his desk.

# Chapter 19

The man was furious. He stormed around the dark room, knocking over everything he could reach along the way. How could she do this to him? How could she learn so quickly to block him out?

He stormed over to the window to peer out through the cracks between the boards. There has to be a way to get back in complete control. He had her relaxed and dreaming. He was setting her mind at peace. She would soon forget all that had happened over the last few months and go on with life so that he could finish his plan. How could he accomplish this? Would he have to bring her back here?

He walked back across the room and started picking up his mess.

He would have to get things ready just in case he needed to bring her back here. How would he handle it if he did? He would have to retrain her. He would have to find ways to get her to stay under his control; to keep her from remembering. But how? Her fear of him kept her pliable, ready, controllable. He picked the rope up and placed it in the seat of the chair. He picked up a blanket and laid it on the seat as well.

He then walked over to the mattress and rubbed his hand across the bloodstains. He would have to think of new adventures for the two of them to share. New ways to prove he had control. How could he influence those around her?

He sat down on the mattress to concentrate. As he did, he wrung his hands around his wrists to feel the pain. He had to clear his mind.

He had to find those around her. He had to.

# Chapter 20

Paige woke with a jolt. "NO!" she screamed. Jay ran from his office to hers.

"Are you okay?" he said as he grabbed her.

"What happened?" she asked. "Did I fall asleep?"

"It looks like it. I can see the drool on your sleeve," he chuckled at her.

Embarrassed, Paige glanced down at her arm and then wiped off her cheek. "I was dreaming. It was only a dream," she breathed deeply, trying to relax.

"What was it, Paige?" he knelt beside her and pulled her closer to him.

Paige let out another deep breath. "I was dreaming of being back in the dark room. Looking at the window, I saw when I fainted at Aileen's," her lips trembling as she spoke, feeling the chill rush up her spine. Jay wanted to kiss them to make them stop, but refrained and resigned himself to just holding her.

"You are remembering, aren't you?" he asked her as she welcomed his arms around her. She could only nod and let herself be held for a few moments, feeling his arms around her. Thinking about how safe he made her feel, she wondered why she couldn't trust him enough to tell him everything. She wanted to but felt it was safer to keep it all inside, at least for now. If she was going to struggle with her own sanity, she didn't need to drag anyone else along with her.

"Come on Paige, let's get out of here and go where we can talk." As he took her arm, he laid the newspaper he still had in his hand on the desk. Paige looked at the picture of David and the blonde woman.

"I guess you are thinking the same thing I did when I first saw it," she pointed at the blonde. She wasn't sure if she wanted his reply.

"It doesn't necessarily mean anything, Paige. It could just be a fan."

Jay secretly hoped that was not the case then felt incredibly guilty for it.

"Does it really look like just a fan to you? Why would she be hiding her face if it was just a fan?" Tears started to swell in her eyes.

He rubbed her arm and led her out of the office and to his car. The sun was shining brightly, but the temperature was very chilly. Fall had its full grip on the weather today and it chilled Paige to the bone.

After stopping at a drive-thru to pick up a couple of burgers, Jay drove to a nearby park to eat at a picnic table near the Ohio River.

Even though the weather was cold, Paige thought it was a good idea.

Maybe the cool air would help clear her mind and help her figure out what was going on.

"Okay, are you going to come clean with me or not?" he asked her just as she took a big mouthful of cheeseburger.

Paige held up one finger and chewed. The mouthful at least gave her a moment to think about what he had just asked her. *"What the heck,"* she thought to herself.

They talked again about the visions she had seen of the dark room. She finally told him about the dream of being tied to a chair and the man that was there. Reluctantly, she told him about the man she kept seeing that seemed to be following her. Everything spilled from her like a waterfall with the exception of one thing. She still didn't tell him about Junna. It all still seemed to be a bit farfetched for even her to believe. Not ready to share that yet, she decided that she needed to think about it some more. Paige felt the need to figure out what she was going to do with what Junna had told her and whether or not she believed her.

"Paige, come stay with me for a few days. You need someone around while you rest. In case you remember something else. Maybe I can help you put the pieces together," Jay begged her.

Paige thought about it for a moment. It would be nice to have someone around whenever something happened. But the independent Paige would rather handle this alone. What if Jay would think she was crazy? Paige was beginning to believe she was really crazy herself.

"I don't know, Jay. I don't want to be a burden to you." She did feel thankful that he wanted to be around her. Maybe she didn't do anything to make him try to avoid her. Maybe all of that was in her head too. Her head began to swim with all of the thoughts, doubts, and fears. Uncertain of Jay's true feelings or intentions, she would rather leave him out of it.

"Oh, come on. You need me and I want to be there for you," he pleaded knowing what he really wanted to be.

Paige hesitated for a moment longer. Too many strange things have happened recently and it would be a good idea to have him around. He had always been a great friend and a partner that she had counted on and highly respected for years. With a big sigh, she decided to agree.

"On one condition, that we stay at my place and you sleep in the extra bedroom and not the couch," she demanded, trying to force a smile.

"Deal!" he smiled at her and shook her hand to seal the contract.

Paige laughed and immediately felt better. "Oh, wait! I do have one more thing. You have to promise me that you will talk to me. You have to tell me everything. I can't help you if you hold things back. Can I make that an amendment to the deal?" he cocked his head sideways and looked at her with a silly grin.

"Okay, amended deal," Paige reluctantly took his hand again. She glanced out over the Ohio River. How could she tell him about Junna and what she had told her? She needed to think and clear her mind.

"Do you mind if I take a short walk along the river? By myself?" she asked him.

"Go ahead," he squeezed her hand and she stood to walk away. He watched her as she walked along the bank. She paused to stare across the river, touching the leaves on the trees as she passed. How beautiful she is, he thought, with her long brown hair blowing in the breeze. Jay realized he was completely in love with her and had just better accept that fact. He knew he couldn't have her and would always be only her friend and partner. *"Well, dammit. I will be the best friend and partner she's ever had."* He resigned himself to loving her from a distance but actively being in her life. He realized that the hardest part of life is missing someone when they are right beside you and you can't have them. *"I'll take whatever I can get,"* he thought to himself, but he knew in his heart he wanted more. He wanted to touch her, kiss her, and hold her. He could never have her. Maybe in time, he'd accept that as well. He hoped so.

Jay then looked up and down the banks for someone, anyone else.

There were other women around. Some of them were playing with their dogs, some just walking, but most with their significant others.

His eyes kept returning to Paige. After rubbing his head a moment, he returned to his cheeseburger. Only she could hold his attention right now and he decided that would probably take some time to accept as well.

# Chapter 21

Junna tried to collect her thoughts. She was taking a risk by contacting Paige. *"What if I slip?"* she asked herself. *"What if he sees what I am thinking? He will if I don't stop asking questions!"* She was doing exactly what she knew better than to do and set out to keep her mind clear.

She needed to concentrate to accomplish anything. Paige had to be ready before she could see her again. She wondered if she had already told her too much and if he knew what she had done already. She couldn't find him. He was blocking himself more and more lately. That worried Junna. Could he be figuring things out?

She got up and paced around her living room, touching her crystal animal figurines that were lined up across the top of her entertainment center. She then felt the softness of the mink lined pillows she used to decorate her couch. She turned to sit and relax.

Taking a deep breath, she tried to concentrate on Paige. She could tell Paige was clearing her mind and could feel her but could not understand what was going on inside of her. "Good," she said out loud.

"Keep that up. I will be able to visit you soon." She kept stroking the pillows gently, concentrating.

Junna then got back up from the sofa and walked over to a table by an open window with a view of the Ohio River. Opening the drawer, she selected a stick of sandalwood incense. She lit the stick and blew out the flame. As she inhaled the pleasant aroma, she walked back to the sofa and sat down to relax and meditate. She knew what she needed to do next. She had to go see Paige again.

# Chapter 22

Paige wandered along the bank of the river, looking at the glistening sunshine across the water and watching as the birds flew overhead searching for food. She felt the leaves in her hands as she touched the trees and walked over to touch the bark. It felt wonderful to enjoy how something looks and feels, realizing that she hadn't taken time for that in a long time. She glanced over her shoulder to look at Jay and wondered what he was thinking. She closed her eyes and concentrated on him. As if she could hear him talking beside her, he said, *"Well, dammit. I will be the best friend and partner she's ever had."* Paige smiled as she opened her eyes to look at him. He was rubbing his face with both hands and watching her. She suddenly realized how much she wanted him around.

"After all, he is very handsome and caring. He's been a great friend," she whispered out loud, daring herself to say the words knowing that she had to keep the words out of her head to keep them private. She rubbed the tree bark again, keeping her mind blank.

After a few moments, she walked back to the picnic

table and sat beside of him. Taking his chin in her hand, she kissed him lightly on the cheek. "Thank you for everything you've done for me," she smiled sweetly at him.

Jay looked deep into her eyes. She felt a knot form in her stomach when she realized he wanted to kiss her. As she ran her thumb along his cheek, he reached out to touch her face. She quickly drew in a breath as he leaned toward her and kissed her lightly. His kiss was soft and sweet, barely touching her lips, arousing every sensation Paige could possibly have. Breathless, she immediately responded and kissed him more passionately, causing Jay to moan softly. Jay felt like he would explode if he couldn't have her now. They both stopped immediately as if a gunshot had gone off.

"Paige, I'm so sorry. I didn't mean to," he tried to say as he fought to regain his breath.

"It's okay Jay," she tried to comfort him. "Really."

"No, I shouldn't have … you are such a great friend … and you have David …"

"Stop!" she cut him off. "If I didn't want you to kiss me, I would not have let you. It's okay. We are still friends aren't we?" she touched his hand.

"Yes, definitely," he said in a low, soft voice. He knew he was not handling this well but decided to give up on trying to regain his dignity.

"Come on, we need to get back to work," he took her hand and walked back to the car.

"Wait, please," she stopped him. "Jay, it's really okay. Don't run away from me. We both got a little carried away."

"I know. I'm sorry. I need to control myself better. I don't want to take advantage of you," he patted her hand as if she were a child.

"Me either," she said. Things now made perfect sense as to why he had been avoiding her.

After returning to the station, it took Paige a while to get her bearings and get back to work. She studied the files and the pictures of Anthony's crime scene again. As she was taking in all of the details of the room, she noticed one picture. Within the photograph, she could see a reflection of herself in the mirror. She was smiling. How strange? She didn't remember smiling. Maybe Jay made some offhand comment that struck her as funny. He was excellent at that sometimes and in the strangest of situations. She shrugged it off. Maybe she was fighting back the nausea that had been consuming her from the time she arrived at the Steckler estate that day. Pacing back and forth in her office, she decided to take another walk and think about the case.

The street was noisy as cars zoomed past. Paige walked along the sidewalk and started toward the Heine Brother's Coffee shop. She felt the cool breeze sweep across her face and she could feel her cheeks turn red. A strong cup of coffee could help clear her head. She opened the door and listened to the bell ring as she approached the counter.

She ordered her coffee and asked for vanilla flavoring. She added her usual ton of cream and sugar then sat down at a small table in the corner. Slowly, she picked up the paper that was on the table to see the picture of David and the woman. Studying the woman, she tried to figure out if she knew her. All she could see was the long, straight, blonde hair. She immediately felt guilty for wondering about her when she had just kissed Jay. Not being convinced, she kept trying to tell herself that Jay's kiss was one of complete friendship and how he just really cares for her. She justified it by telling herself that it was because he is just lonely right now and needed something to make himself feel better. And so was she. There had been enough emotion between the two of them in the last few months to justify any feelings they had at that particular moment.

After glancing around the coffee shop, she took a deep breath and looked at the picture again. Something seemed familiar about the blonde hair. But then again, how many women are there with long, straight, blonde hair? She managed to laugh. It seemed most successful men had one of those blondes on his hip. Maybe David was the same way. Did he want one now that he was becoming a success?

"May I join you?" she heard a small voice from above her. She looked up to find Junna standing there.

"Sure," Paige smiled at her. "I hoped I'd see you again. I have a lot of questions."

"I'm sure you do," Junna sat across from her as she looked around to see if anyone was watching. "You have been doing a great job clearing you mind, Paige. I think you are ready to hear more."

"First, I have to know one thing," Paige said flatly. "What are your motives?"

Smiling, Junna replied, "I can't tell you all of them all just yet. But I will tell you that I honestly just want to help you. I have to help you, Paige. I couldn't live with myself if I didn't."

Paige looked at her and believed that she looked genuinely concerned. *"But why? Why would Junna be concerned with me?"* she thought.

"Because I care about you, Paige," she said. "Be careful what you think."

Paige realized that she had just been read. She took a drink of her coffee and rubbed her napkin between her fingertips, feeling the texture. She had to believe her now. "Okay, go ahead."

"There is a lot I need to tell you. A lot you will not be able to think about. I'm not sure you will believe me, but I have to tell you. So I'll start with this …" Junna took a deep breath and let it out slowly.

"Someone wants to hurt you. They are using you for what they want. Paige," she hesitated, "he is the one that took you. He has not let you go."

Paige felt as if she were hit by a dump truck. "You know who he is? Tell me!"

"I can't," Junna looked down at the table. "I just know he has not given you up. He's continually reading you."

"How do you know this? Are you working with him?"

"No … *no!*" Junna pleaded. "You will just have to trust me. I need to help you."

"You are making it difficult. How can I trust you when you are telling me you know about my kidnapping and that he is still reading me, but you won't tell me who he is?"

"I can't!" Junna began to cry. "I just have to tell you how to stop him from controlling you. I have to show you how to remember. I'm not as strong as he is. He'd kill me if he even knew I spoke to you."

"So you do know who he is!" Paige's voice was getting louder.

"Stop it, Paige. He'll know! I don't even know where he is!" At the sound of the urgency in her voice, Paige calmed down. Junna was truly terrified.

"I'm sorry. Junna, I'll be quiet and listen." Paige reached out and touched her hand. She was genuinely concerned.

After dabbing at the area under her eyes with a napkin, Junna continued. "Do you ever feel like someone is telling you to calm down and that things will be fine?"

Paige nodded as she remembered thinking she was going crazy in the shower.

"Don't listen to him, Paige. When you feel like you are being told to do something that is against your nature to do, fight back. Don't let him know you are fighting back. Just clear your mind. Ignore the suggestions. He is a far better reader than I am. He cannot only tap into the collective conscious, but he can also control it by adding suggestions.

When he is reading your thoughts, he can suggest a thought back to you. He can make you think it is your decision to do or say anything.

You have to learn the difference. He can't control how you feel, only suggest what to think. If you need to think and reason through something, say it out loud. Your thoughts then become part of your surroundings and not the collective conscious. That is what separates the two. He has to be beside you to overhear you to understand." Junna smiled a little. "Yes, I'm telling you to talk to yourself. Just make sure you are alone when you do."

Paige sat in silence for a moment. "How do I know you aren't doing the same?"

"That is for you to believe. I won't try to make you. I'm not like him."

Junna stood up to walk away. "I'm here for you, Paige. I want to help you. Your memories will come back to you if you block him long enough. He is keeping you from remembering."

"How is he keeping me from remembering?"

Junna paused and leaned toward her. "When you start thinking about some things, you start to feel sick to your stomach don't you?"

"Yes," Paige said as she remembered all of the nausea.

"He puts the thought in your head that you feel sick. That then makes you sick."

"How do you know all of this? How will I find you if I have more questions?"

"I can't tell you everything yet. It's too big of a risk. I

can only give you the tools you need to fight him. You have to Paige. Before it's too late," she started to walk away.

"Wait, Junna ... how will I find you?" Paige pleaded, not satisfied with the answer.

"I will find you." With that said, she walked out the door.

Paige sighed deeply while she watched Junna disappear from sight.

As she looked around the coffee shop again, she spotted Ian out of the corner of her eye. He was sitting at a small table in the darkest area of the shop, watching her. When he caught her glance, he looked down and pretended to read the book he had in front of him. "What are you up to, little man?" Paige whispered as she stood and walked out of the shop, glancing back at him as she let the door shut behind her.

# Chapter 23

"Junna! You little bitch!" he screamed. "I'll have your head for this!" He paced around the dark room, knowing he could rant out loud without thinking the words. "So, you've been reading me! All this time, you are a reader too! I can see Paige thinking about you. You just think you've ruined everything for me."

"I'll get her back. She's not strong. She's learning to block me, but she can't keep that up for long. No one can," he smiled. He'd just have to work harder. After all, he loved a challenge. He knew Paige had doubts about Junna. He would just have to change strategies. This is not anything he couldn't handle. No one is as strong as he. He paced the floor talking to himself on what to do next. He meditated on Paige and tried to find her thoughts. He could feel her but couldn't understand.

He ranted about Junna. How did she figure it out? How long had she read him?

He angrily kicked the chair across the room and it shattered into several pieces. He walked over to it and picked up the rope. He admired the bloodstains that were matted throughout its length. "I think it's time to add yours," he smiled maliciously and walked out of the door.

# Chapter 24

Junna ran home to pack her things, knowing that she had to go somewhere else, anywhere else and she knew she couldn't think ahead about it. He knew where she lived and it wasn't safe anymore.

Paige knew too much now. She hurried around her house, grabbing everything she could stuff in one suitcase and tried to zip the bag shut. After fighting the zipper for a few moments, she gave up, held it together and ran for the door. Fear stopped her cold when she saw the door was open. Had she left it open when she ran in? She looked around the living room until she was satisfied that no one came in after her and walked to the door. Cautiously, she peered outside.

The shrubs looked undisturbed, there were birds in the yard, and her neighbors were going about their business with their yard work. Still not convinced that everything was fine, she slowly walked to her car, looking in all directions along the way.

Thinking it must be safe; she ran for the car and threw her bag in the front passenger seat. After starting her car and squealing down the street, she started to relax a little. Slowly, she caught her breath.

Knowing she was better not to think of where she was going, she drove on and on. If she drove long enough, she could find someplace safe and not think about where that was. She turned on the radio so that she could just listen and clear her mind. When her favorite song came on, she sang at the top of her lungs. Trying to do anything she could to not think about where she was going. After taking several exits onto different expressways, she finally pulled off onto a side road. She tried not to pay attention to where the road went and just drove on and on.

Static from the radio station had Junna scanning for another one. When she looked up from the radio, she could see something from her back seat in her rearview mirror. Terror overtook her as she saw his eyes leering at her. Those cold gray eyes that were all too familiar.

Junna's heart was pounding in her throat.

"Junna, you have something to tell me," his icy voice whispered over her shoulder. "Junna, you have been a very bad ... bad ... girl."

She felt the ice from his voice trail up and down her spine as she tried to swallow her thumping heart, but was unable. She felt his hand touch her neck and felt the cold steel of a handgun on her throat. "Pull over, little Junna. Be a good girl and pull over quietly."

She pulled the car to the side of the road and realized she was on a country road where no one would find her if he left her there. Panic took over so that she could barely move a muscle.

"Now, slowly get out of the car," he whispered sweetly in her ear.

His voice was calm and slow, which only heightened the fear in Junna.

She opened her door as he opened his behind her and slowly got out.

He pushed her face first against the car. "Put your hands behind your back ... *Now!*" he screamed when she didn't respond immediately.

Shaking badly, Junna did what she was told. She felt him tie her hands together and could taste the tears as they fell across her lips but she didn't make a sound. She only felt and tasted and listened to his voice. "How did you learn to block a reader, dear Junna? For that matter, how long have you known you were one?" He traced the barrel along her cheekbone. "Speak to me or I'll pull this trigger and leave your pretty little brain all over this pretty little car!"

"Since I was very young. Like you," she whispered breathlessly through the tears that now drenched her mouth. She tried to look around to see if maybe, just maybe, someone was near. There was not a house in sight and no traffic on the road. Her plan had failed. She had given him the perfect place to take care of her. He could leave her here and no one would ever be able to find her.

"Why didn't you say anything?" He continued to trace the gun along her cheekbone and pushed her harder against the car. She could feel him tighten the rope around her hands.

"I wasn't sure. Not for quite a while." As soon as Junna tried to turn and look at him, he slammed her head into the car. "What are you going to do to me?" she managed to mutter after the stars cleared from her sight.

"I'll ask the questions," he pulled her away from the car and pushed her into the back seat.

As he started to drive away, he asked, "How many people have you read?"

"Not, not a lot. It didn't feel right to me, nosing into other people's personal thoughts," she sniffed.

"That's just it. They are not personal. Not if you know where to look. Nothing is personal. Nothing is sacred anymore," his voice hissed through the car.

"What are you going to do?" she begged.

He snapped. "I told you! I'll ask the questions!" Junna's heart leaped back into her throat. "How much do you know?"

"A … about what?"

"Don't be coy with me! I know you've told Paige about me," his voice becoming more agitated.

"You seem to know everything. Why should I have to tell you?"

"You're right. And there's not a damn thing you can do about anything now, is there?" Junna felt helpless. She had hurt Paige more than she helped.

# Chapter 25

Paige broke her promise. She didn't tell Jay about everything. She left out all of the details about Junna. She wasn't ready for that yet. They had dinner last night talking about baseball and the upcoming World Series. They avoided all of the awkward glances they were casting each other. Jay finally suggested they go shopping. Paige agreed. That would be the perfect way to have fun and keep her mind off of things.

When they pulled up to the mall, Jay made her wait in the car for a moment while he ran around to open her door. This made Paige smile.

No one had done that for her in quite a while. Even David with all of his manners never opened the car door for her when she got out of the car, only to let her in.

"My lady," Jay smiled sweetly and held out his arm for Paige to take as she stepped out of the car.

"Why, thank you ever so much!" Paige added a thick southern drawl and sweetly placed her arm through his.

"It's really getting chilly," he added as he pulled her closer to him to block the brisk breeze that was blowing across the parking lot. "It will be snowing soon!"

"Don't remind me. I hate snow!" The thought sent chills down her spine.

They hurried on into the mall and started browsing from store to store. They looked at printed t-shirts and made fun of all the quotes and pictures on them.

"I think I'll get this one for my mother!" Jay exclaimed as he held up a shirt that had an image of a lady in a bikini and read *I'm one Sexy Momma*.

"I'm sure she would appreciate it." Paige laughed. "How is she anyway?"

"She's doing very well. She's back to pestering me about getting married. She says she's getting too old to become a grandmother; like anyone is too old to be a grandmother!" Jay shuffled his feet on the floor.

"Maybe someday all of those kids you've fathered through the years will crawl out of the woodwork and hunt you down. You could really surprise her!" Paige chuckled and punched him on the arm.

"They'd have to catch me first," he cast a handsome smile her way.

As Paige took a step back, she bumped into someone. As she turned to apologize, she realized it was Ian.

"Ian," she said curtly.

"Ms. Aldridge," he replied, nodded and continued with his shopping.

Paige looked at Jay and shrugged her shoulders.

Paige and Jay shopped around for a while as she kept an eye on Ian.

He shuffled around the racks, picking out something occasionally just to put it right back on the rack again.

She picked up a couple of things as a head start on Christmas gifts before deciding to go home to get some rest.

Paige didn't sleep at all well. She considered everything Junna had said to her. Trying not to think about it was impossible. She tried to only say things out loud like Junna had suggested, but she was afraid Jay would overhear her and think she had fallen off her rocker. Harry lay on the foot of the bed, watching her toss and turn. He let out a groan of disapproval.

Paige laughed at him and patted his head. "Okay, I'll think about something else then," she shut her eyes and tried to concentrate on the dream she had about the waterfall and soon fell asleep.

When Paige and Jay went in to work the next morning, Hannah met them at the door. "I'm glad you two are finally here. There's been a break-in at the Steckler's estate. You'd better get over there now. The chief didn't want me to radio you, but I thought you would want to know," Hannah ran out of breath from talking so fast.

"We'd better go!" Jay said as he took Paige's arm and headed for the car.

"What was that all about?" Paige asked as she buckled her seatbelt.

"I don't know. That was kind of strange. Why wouldn't the chief want us to know? And why would Hannah tell us anyway?" Puzzled, Jay drove on toward the estate. Paige tried not to think of what it could be now. So much had happened in the last few weeks.

"Maybe this is the break we've been looking for? You know? A return to the scene of the crime type of thing?" Paige declared.

"I hope so," Jay said optimistically.

When they arrived, police cars were still in the driveway. The house had been empty since the auction. Even though it now belonged to Paige, she hadn't been in it since. The memories were too hard to face and the house still felt like death to her. She had thought about selling the house but realized that it would not sell until some of the press had died down.

The glass in the front door was broken where

someone had obviously forced their way in leaving a trail of broken glass through the entranceway. As Paige made her way across the glass into the parlor, she saw it. Spray painted in red across the wall was the phrase *"Death to you all"*.

"Oh my God," Paige whispered as she placed her hand over her mouth. As she sank down onto the floor, Jay stopped in his tracks behind her.

He knelt beside her and took her hand. "You okay?" he asked.

She could only shake her head. "Oh my God," she said again.

Jay looked back up at the letters. "Are there any witnesses?" he asked Tom, one of the other detectives, who was standing over them.

"Yes, Jay, you had better come with me. Adam, stay with Paige," he patted the other officer on the shoulder.

Reluctantly, Jay stood up and walked outside with Tom. Paige, still sitting in the middle of the broken glass, began to rock back and forth, tears welling in her eyes.

Tom whispered to Jay, "One of the neighbors saw a woman dressed in black running from the estate just after midnight. They didn't get a good enough look to be able to tell more than that. She ran two houses down, that way," he pointed down the street, "hopped onto a motorcycle and disappeared."

Jay rubbed his chin. "What is going on around here?"

"That's a very good question. I didn't want Paige to come over here and see this. I'm afraid for her, Jay," Tom looked very concerned. What if she's next?"

"I'll stay with her … night and day if I have to," Jay whispered, looking back in at Paige. He was determined to protect her. He fought the urge to run in, hold her in his arms and take her away from all of this.

"That's what I was going to suggest," Tom sighed

nervously, rubbing his hands together. He had no idea that Jay was already with Paige day and night.

Jay turned and walked back to Paige, who had stood up and was touching the spray paint. Her eyes were closed as she was concentrating on the writing. She rubbed her hand across the wall as if feeling the letters would help her understand what happened.

"What is it, Paige?" Jay asked quietly as he walked up behind her.

"You wouldn't believe me if I told you," she continued sweeping her hands across the letters.

"Try me." He walked closer to her so she could whisper.

"Just give me a few minutes. I'm trying to read who did this. I'm trying to listen to them," she opened her eyes and turned toward him, her eyes pleading for understanding. Confused, Jay nodded and stepped back away from her.

Paige continued with her ritualistic behavior. She whispered to herself, "Where are you? Who are you? Why are you doing this?" She kept repeating this over and over. She visualized the can of red spray paint in her hand and hearing the words, *"Yes, that's it. Yes, that's it,"* in her head. "The paint was in my hands," she barely whispered. Suddenly, she felt ill and swayed against the wall.

Jay ran to her and put his arm around her shoulders. "Okay. Now are you ready to talk?"

Paige shifted her concentration to Jay. She looked at him and could hear him plead with her, *"Please talk to me, Paige!"* His mouth hadn't moved. Looking back at the wall she concentrated more and could hear him say, *"God Paige, I love you. Please talk to me!"*

She turned back to him. "The only way I can make you believe this is to say one thing," she took a deep breath and said, "I just heard you say you love me." She closed her eyes drew in another deep breath.

What if she only heard what she wanted to hear and not what he thought? He would think she was crazy. When she opened her eyes again and faced him, he had the look of total astonishment. So much so, that his mouth was wide open. Paige knew it was true. She had read him.

# Chapter 26

After answering questions about who her enemies might be, telling the officers that she could not remember her kidnapper, and she knew of no other enemies, Paige led Jay to the car. He looked as disheveled as she felt. She still had told no one about Junna or about seeing the can of spray paint in her hand. "That will come, if he will listen," she whispered just out of Jay's earshot.

"I'll explain when we get home," she said as she pat his hand.

Jay tried to understand, although he desperately wanted to know what had just happened. *"Had he said it out loud? He was sure he hadn't. What was Paige doing while looking at the spray-painted words? Why was she behaving so strangely? Why did she seem to have more composure than he did right now? What the hell is going on here?"* The questions kept circling in his mind, over and over again. Every time, sounding like new questions.

They rode in silence all the way home.

When they arrived, David was waiting by the door.

"Hey, baby!" he said as she walked up. "Hi, Jay."

Jay only nodded. "Hey!" Paige smiled at him.

"Paige, I really need to talk to you. Can we have a few minutes alone?" David asked, looking at Jay.

"Sure," she unlocked the door.

"Go on in and help yourself to something to drink," she told Jay as she held the door open for him and Harry ran outside.

She then turned to David. "I wasn't expecting you back so soon," she said as she hugged him tightly.

"I wasn't expecting to be back. I wanted to see you and talk to you," he said as he sat down and motioned for her to sit on the glider beside him.

Paige could tell this wasn't going to be a good conversation and immediately knew what it was about. She took the seat beside him and took a deep breath. "It's about the woman in the paper."

"Yes," David shuffled his feet on the porch. "I knew you would figure it out so I thought I should come and talk to you myself. I want to …"

"Before you begin, I was giving you the benefit of the doubt. The paper mentioned nothing about her. I wasn't going to concern myself with it," she stood and walked to the end of her porch.

"I wanted to tell you sooner, but you were going through so much," he said as he walked up behind her. They stood in silence for a moment as Paige stared off across the neighborhood.

"It's okay … really. You've always been there for me and I haven't been there for you in a long time. I know that. I understand and I guess I've expected it for some time," she said breathlessly. She could feel the puzzled expression on David's face even though her back was to him.

"I didn't expect you to take this so well. Aileen was afraid you would freak out."

"Aileen? That was Aileen?" Paige began to tremble as she turned to face him.

"I'm sorry. I thought you had figured that out as well," he said as he turned his back to her and looked at the sky. Paige felt as if someone had punched her in the stomach.

"No, that part just bowled me over!" Paige then fought back the tears. Not only had her boyfriend, but her family betrayed her as well. She thought she recognized the woman in the paper. "Aileen," she walked out into the yard and paced back and forth, muttering the word over and over again as if it would suddenly make sense.

"I see that part is bothering you more," David turned back to her and followed her out into the yard. "I'm so sorry, Paige. I didn't want to hurt you." David reached toward her as she away.

"It's okay. I'm strong. I'll get over it. I'm worried about Jones. I'm assuming he knows," Paige said as she put her hand on her hip as if to give David a lecture on tearing up marriages.

"I know you will. You can handle anything. And yes, he knows. Aileen is talking to him now as well. I'll miss you, Paige," David kissed her on the head and started to walk away. Paige stood in the yard for a few moments.

"How long?" she yelled after him. "How long has this been going on?"

He turned back to face her. "Since just before Anthony was murdered. Like I said, you've had so much going on that I couldn't tell you."

Dumbfounded, Paige responded, "I stayed at her home. She treated me like a friend, not just like family. Like the family we've tried to be over the years!" Rage began to take over. She started pacing back and forth, breathing heavily. Tears started to streak down her face. "I hate you … I hate you both!" she screamed at him.

"Get off my property you lying, cheating son of a bitch! I hope you rot in hell! You both deserve it!"

David just turned and walked away. She watched him with eyes full of tears and hatred as he climbed into his car and drove away. Her stomach clenched in a knot that she thought she could not break free from. Trembling with rage, she looked around the yard and caught a glimpse of her neighbor peaking out of their window. She paced a moment longer, not caring what the neighbors thought.

She talked out loud, "I'm going crazy. I'm talking to myself, hearing voices, seeing visions. I'm going crazy." She continued to pace. Tears were pouring down her face now. She wiped them with the sleeve of her jacket and stood in the cold air for a while longer. Now she had to go in to face Jay. He would think she was crazy too, but she needed to explain what had just happened.

Paige turned around and could see Jay sitting at the kitchen table. Breathing deeply, she gathered her courage and went in. At least she knew she had his friendship and she knew she had his love. Would he still love her after hearing everything? It was a chance she had to take. She didn't have a choice any longer.

# Chapter 27

Paige slowly told Jay about Junna. She told him about the readers and about what Junna had said about her kidnapping. He just listened.

He didn't nod or give any other acknowledgment of what she was saying. Finally, he stood and walked across the room as Paige just watched him. He paced back and forth in the kitchen. His mind was racing, mostly in disbelief. Wanting desperately to wake up from this nightmare he pinched himself. "I can't believe this," he muttered continually. Crossing his arms and drumming his fingers on his elbows, he continued to pace. His emotions were bouncing from anger to wanting to kiss Paige, to wanting to slug David for upsetting her now. He had watched them from the window enough to know David had hurt her, but he didn't understand how he felt about anything for certain so he continued to pace.

After watching him for some time, Paige walked to him and touched his shoulder.

He wheeled around and looked at her, "Are you reading me now?"

Stunned she took a step back. For a second she was relieved to know he believed her and then disappointed that he seemed aggravated at the thought that she could read him. Her heart was pounding in her ears while it rested in her throat.

"No, I wasn't trying to," she whispered as tears started to form, yet again, in her eyes.

"How many times have you read me?" His demeanor was cold.

"I don't know. A couple of times I thought I had but wasn't sure. I wasn't trying to until tonight. I took a chance tonight by telling you that. I was afraid I was forming words in my head of what I thought I wanted to hear from you." Paige was feeling defensive now and still afraid. He would think she was crazy and would want to leave her alone. Who could blame him? "I'm sure you think I'm crazy," she finally whispered and turned her back to him. Tears began to swell now and fall down her cheeks.

"Why didn't you tell me any of this before?" His voice was still cold.

She hesitated. "I didn't want you to think I was off my rocker. Hell, I think I'm off my rocker now! I'm hearing voices, seeing people," exasperated, she paced around the kitchen with her hands in her hair, squeezing her head.

He reached up and touched her face. "Read me, Paige. Read me now," he said, finally confident of what he was feeling.

She closed her eyes and concentrated, worried that she would not be able to read on demand. Trying to relax and breathe slowly, she turned her entire attention on him, attempting to find him in the collective conscious. Words formed in her head as she heard him say, *"Paige, I do love you. I do believe you."*

"I'm afraid to say," she was crying harder now as she

looked at him.

"Paige, I do *not* love you," he said this time out loud.

Astonished, Paige turned from him. "You didn't say 'not' in your mind, or did you?"

Jay laughed out loud. "Okay, so I love you. Just don't tell David okay?"

"He has Aileen now," she was looking at him again as the anger started to rebuild.

"You are full of surprises tonight. What do you mean?" he said as he motioned for her to sit down at the kitchen table, knowing that was what the argument outside was about.

"That's what he came by here to tell me. The woman in the paper is Aileen. They are together now. Evidently Jones knows too," sighing, she rested her head in her hands, trying to choke down the bitter anger that was building like bile in the back of her throat.

"Are you okay?" he asked her; feeling a little dumbfounded.

"I'm fine. The only surprise was that it was Aileen." She took his hand in hers, "I was expecting it to happen. It's been different for a while now. I'm just upset about Aileen; all of the lies. I feel like such an idiot. Why didn't I see it? I feel so betrayed by both of them, especially Aileen. How could she do this to me?" Paige stood to pace the room.

The pain of it all had built up so much inside that she started to sob uncontrollably, trying to find some sort of release.

"Paige, take a breath," Jay pleaded as he pulled her to him. "Do you need some time alone?"

"The first thing I saw when he left was you sitting at my kitchen table," she paused. "I felt like you belonged there. I need you. I've never been able to admit to needing anyone, but I need you. I need you here with me!"

"I belong wherever you are," he pulled her to him and kissed her lightly. He held on to her and let her rest her head on his shoulder.

"I know you are confused and vulnerable right now, but I'm here for you."

"I do want some time before anything more happens between us. So you don't think I'm using you to get over David. Hell, so I don't think I'm using you to get over David," she said softly as she touched his cheek.

"I feel the same way. I won't take advantage of you right now. I love you too much."

"I already know that," she wiped her face with her hands and kissed him again.

"We'll get you some help, I promise you that. We'll find out what is going on," he tried to reassure her. At the same time, attempted to reassure himself.

# Chapter 28

Junna woke to find herself tied to the chair. She could smell the blood that was dried on her face and she felt sick. Trying not to think about what was happening to her, she looked around the room. She could see the window; the window she'd seen in Paige's dreams. Biting her lip, she tried to concentrate on Paige but since she had been working on blocking a reader, she couldn't find Paige in her thoughts. Occasionally, she caught glimpses of her thinking about Jay and David. Junna's heart broke at all of the pain she was going through at this time. How could she reach out to her? She had to find a way.

"Paige, I'm so sorry," she said out loud. "How much more can you bear?" Junna took a deep breath. Paige needed to be warned somehow.

He was coming after her. She tried to figure out how to concentrate on Paige without him reading her every thought. Tears poured down her face. What could she do? Junna felt utterly helpless. She whispered, "Paige, I'm sorry I failed you. God, I hope you are alright."

It was dark outside and Junna could barely see the

stars through a crack between the boards on the window. Clouds slowly moved across them to block her view. Speaking softly, she repeated over and over again, "If there is a God in heaven, please help her. She doesn't deserve this."

# Chapter 29

Jay crawled out of his bed in Paige's spare room and called into the police station. He told the captain that he and Paige were going to take the day off. The captain said he understood. Jay then poked his head in Paige's room to see if she was still asleep. After pausing long enough to watch her sleep, he stepped outside on the porch to call Dr. Southerland.

"Hello Jeffrey, this is Jay Vittadini. I really need to talk to you."

"Sure Jay, what's going on?" Dr. Southerland asked.

Jay explained what had been happening to a friend of his and wondered what could be going on. He explained everything except for the collective conscious.

"Well Jay, I can't say for sure without seeing your friend, and this is in no way a diagnosis. But I will say this; it sounds like it could be schizophrenia," he paused and cleared his throat. "The typical symptoms of schizophrenia include visual and auditory hallucinations.

The sufferer tries to interpret these very realistic hallucinations by developing delusions. One delusion may be that they think they have some sort of magic power or that they are God." He coughed and cleared his throat again. "The most common form is paranoid schizophrenia. This is where the sufferer's thoughts are controlled by strong suspicious delusions like someone is after them or following them and auditory hallucinations or like hearing voices."

Dr. Southerland continued, "The sufferer may also have a form of split personality or Multiple Personality Syndrome. They may cause the personality to split into sub-personalities, also known as alters. The alters have their own memory, and they usually don't know of each other. Consequently, the sufferer has episodes of amnesia whenever an alter has taken over. Some sort of severe abuse, including sexual abuse, usually brings on the development of a split personality.

During the abuse, the person becomes dissociated from the experience. In other words, becomes 'not there', and an alter personality takes over. For every traumatic experience, an alter is created. I would strongly suggest you helping your friend. You can try to get them to see me or I can recommend another doctor if necessary."

"Thank you, Dr. Southerland. I'll do what I can. I don't know how to approach them about it, but I will try." Jay hung up the phone and sank down into the porch swing. He sat outside for quite a while, thinking about what Dr. Southerland had said. He didn't know what to think. He spoke out loud, just in case, "Is Paige schizophrenic? Is that what was going on? Could all of this be a result of her kidnapping?

Could Junna be an alter? Is she paranoid in thinking the man she kept seeing was following her? And the voices? God, I kissed her after all.

She knew I loved her. She hears what others are telling her. Is it all in her mind? Oh, God, she's seen herself do things, the rope, the hands."

Jumping up from the chair, he took off running through the yard until he reached the fence. Not wanting to think she was guilty of anything, he tried to wipe the thought out of his mind. He knew he needed to help her, one way or another. He took a deep breath and decided to go in and check on Paige.

She was still asleep, but not peacefully. Jay looked around the room and saw the journal, laying open on her nightstand and began to read from it.

> *"It's been a day from hell. I'm still having trouble remembering things and the things I can remember, I don't want to. I see things that I shouldn't see and hear things I shouldn't hear. What's wrong with me? Why won't the pieces fit together? I told Jay tonight. I told him everything. He's going to think I'm crazy. Why not? I'm still wondering that myself. Am I? I'm so angry with David and Aileen. How could they do this to me? How could they do this to Jones? I can feel the hate build up inside of me and I don't know how to handle it. If Jay were not here, I don't know what I would do. I am glad he is here and that he loves me. I am afraid of falling asleep, but I know I must. I have to rest so that I can figure everything out."*

She tossed her head from side to side and shot up in the bed screaming. He ran to her and held her to try to calm her down. "What happened? It's a dream, only a dream. What was it about?" he said as he was stroking her long brown hair.

She blinked her eyes and looked at him. "I was in the

room." She was sobbing, her breath leaving her as she spoke. "I was in the room. He was there. I couldn't see him, but I could feel him there. I was killing cats with my bare hands, strangling them. He was watching me … laughing … telling me what a good job I was doing. I couldn't stop. I was so scared. Oh God Jay. What does that mean?" Paige began sobbing hysterically. Jay didn't know what to do. He just held her and let her cry.

"What if it's Junna? What if she is putting these thoughts in your head?" Jay asked her. Paige thought about that for a moment.

"I've considered that. I don't even know where she came from. I've even thought that she said enough to me to make me think these things."

"Did she tell you her last name?" he asked as he rubbed her shoulders.

She was beginning to breathe normally again.

"Yeah… her name is Breck, Junna Breck."

"How hard would it be to track down someone named Junna?" Jay stood up and went to the phone in the living room. Maybe if he could prove she didn't exist, he could convince Paige to go to counseling. She needed help.

Paige looked around her room. "What if it is Junna?" she whispered to herself. She then wondered if Junna was the one who broke into the Steckler Estate and wrote *Death to you all* on the wall. "What are you trying to do to me?" she whispered.

Jay returned to the room. "I have Adam looking into anything he could find on a Junna Breck. We'll see where she's from and if she has a history. We'll find out if she's doing this to you. Meanwhile, I've called in to work for the both of us. We have the day off. What do you say to us getting breakfast somewhere?" he said trying to lighten the mood. He thought again about taking her to see Dr. Southerland. If he could prove that

Junna Breck was not a real person, he may be able to persuade her to go. How could he bring this up without upsetting her?

*"She's so worried that I would think she's crazy,"* he thought to himself. *"But I have to. I have to help."*

"Okay. I just need a quick shower," she sighed as she threw back the covers.

"Take your time," he helped her out of the bed. She looked up at him and kissed him lightly. He smiled, patted her on the shoulder, and sent her on her way to the shower.

# Chapter 30

Paige and Jay decided to have breakfast at Pauline's, a small restaurant on Bardstown Road. Pauline's is a cozy little place that touts southern style breakfasts like scrambled eggs and potatoes served in a hot skillet and grits with biscuits and gravy.

While they were eating, Paige again told him about her dreams and how she felt like she was there, strangling the life out of the helpless kittens. She knew what she was doing was wrong and she didn't want to be doing it, but it seemed beyond her control. She had no control.

"I couldn't stop. I was crying for them, but I still killed them, one by one. What's going on with me?" she asked as she desperately fought back the tears that threatened to flood down her cheeks.

Jay took both of her hands in his. "I don't know, but I am determined to find out. Do you think you were remembering something or was it just a nightmare? Where were you in this dream?"

Paige thought for a moment. "All I remember is a mattress, a bloody mattress, the kind with the blue and white stripes," she motioned up and down with her hands to signify the long lines and to show the width of them with her fingers about three inches apart. "What if I have done those things? What does that mean?"

"Paige, I don't believe you did. You are not capable of doing such a thing."

"Are you sure about that? I'm not anymore," Paige hesitated. She remembered telling Jay about dreaming her hands were around Anthony's neck. Was she capable of killing kittens? Had she killed Anthony? Overwhelming sorrow overtook her and enveloped her with fear. "I need to walk, ..." she whispered as she got up from the table and ran out of the café.

Jay paid the bill and went after her. By the time he stepped outside, she was nowhere in sight. "Paige ..." he shouted up and down the street with no answer. Then he got into his car and drove around.

He couldn't find her anywhere. He decided to go back to her place and wait for her there. *"Maybe she just needed time,"* he thought to himself as he worried about her.

Dazed, Paige walked from corner to corner, up and down alleys, wandering aimlessly, and thinking about her dream. Had she killed Anthony? What about Richie? She envisioned the rope in her hand.

She dreamt of the rope in her hand! "Oh my God!" she screamed as tears poured down her face. She paced in a circle in an alley and sat down by a rusty dumpster. *"I've killed them both. I've killed them both!"* she thought as she curled up in the fetal position and rocked back and forth. "Junna, why did you help me remember this? *Why?* Did I kill Sarah too?" she screamed looking up at the sky as if Junna were looming overhead. She then buried her head between her knees and sobbed so hard she couldn't breathe.

"Paige," a deep voice resonated above her. As Paige looked up, she heard a loud thud as something hit her hard on the head. The world she was in turned black.

# Chapter 31

As Jay arrived at Paige's, John Waters, the Chief of Police was waiting at the door. "Hey John," Jay nodded to him as he walked up.

"Morning, Jay. Where's Paige?" he asked tersely.

"I don't know. We were having breakfast at Pauline's Café when she said she needed to walk. I haven't seen her since. Why? What's up?"

Jay asked as fear began to take over.

"Jay, let's sit down," John said as he pointed to the porch swing. Hesitantly, Jay lowered himself onto the swing. John sat in a chair across from him. "Why did she need to walk?" he asked as he crossed his arms over his chest.

"She had a terrible nightmare that was sticking with her this morning. She needed to clear her head, I guess? What's going on, John?" Jay pleaded with him.

"The Homeowners Association of Gellendale Estates had security cameras installed shortly after the Steckler boy's suicide. We reviewed the tapes," John said as he looked down at his feet while he shuffled them under the chair.

"Go on," Jay was afraid of what was to come next.

"We have the license plate on the motorcycle. It's registered under the name of Jeanne Arozo. She lives right there," he pointed across the yard to Paige's neighbor, the redhead with the Norfolk terrier.

"So we have her then?" Jay asked hopefully, holding his breath.

"There are a couple of things. Miss Arozo was on a plane coming back from Mexico last night. She came home and reported her motorcycle stolen. It was found around the corner." John then stood up and paced across the porch. He took a deep breath and continued.

"The person coming out of the house on the tape looks something like Paige, but we could not see her clearly. It's a bit coincidental that the motorcycle was within reach."

"You don't think Paige would do that, do you?" Jay asked as he stood and walked beside of John.

"I'm not sure yet. It's just that too many things are coming together. Paige's disappearance a couple of years ago, she's really close to the family, has full access. It's amazing she has selective memory during the last couple of years don't you think?"

"You do think she did it? You're crazy man. Paige isn't capable of anything like that!" Jay then remembered her dream of killing the cats.

A big black cloud of doubt formed over him.

"Look, man, I'm sorry. I know she's your partner and all, but even you have enough sense to put two and two together. Can I count on you to help with the rest of the pieces? Can you talk to her and try to figure out what is going on? She may confide in you." John sat back down in the chair, "Keep her here until we figure this out and we can arrest her if the pieces fit."

Jay breathed deeply and sat back down as well. "Sure. We'll figure this out," he whispered as he whole

Lynn Tincher

body began to feel numb.

"There's one more thing," John placed his hand on Jay's arm. "We're trying to keep this out of the press right now. Aileen Childers was found dead near her barn a short time ago. She had been hit in the head with a shovel. Her husband, Jones, found her."

Jay felt as if he were melting through the seat cushion. His head was swimming so fast he thought he would pass out cold. John patted his arm. "I need to get back to the station and file my report. Please keep her here. Don't let on. We'll do what we can to keep our suspicions a secret until we have more information. Let me know when she returns, will ya?" he said as he started down the stairs. "Remember don't say anything to her about Aileen just yet. If it's possible that she's guilty of that one too, we want her to stick around."

Stunned, Jay watched him walk away. Thoughts were racing through his head faster than he had time to process them. How could Paige be capable of these things? The woman he fell in love with is not capable of these things. "But she dreamt of killing cats," he whispered to himself as he stood up from the swing and began to pace around.

"She's a smart girl. Maybe she is setting up an insanity defense? Mind reader? Anyone in their right mind could figure out I love her. Hell, I kissed the woman!"

"What about Junna? I need to know about Junna!" He said to himself as he fumbled for the key that Paige had given him and unlocked the door. He dropped the phone as he reached for it. He picked it back up and dialed the number to the station and asked for Adam.

"Yeah, Jay, how are ya?" Adam answered.

"Have you found out anything on Miss Junna Breck?" Jay waited anxiously for a response.

"Not yet. Our initial research turned up a blank. We

can't find her registered anywhere. But we're still looking and I'll let you know as soon as something has turned up."

Defeated, Jay replied, "Thanks" and hung up the phone. He didn't know if he was glad Junna had not turned up or if he wanted to find her. He decided he hoped he would find her. At least then, maybe Paige would stand a chance. He had to believe she was not guilty and maybe not crazy.

Harry pawed at Jay's leg to get his attention. Jay decided to take him for a walk and try to clear his head. He put Harry on a leash and headed out the door, locking it behind him. As he continued along the street, he noticed Paige's neighbor watching him from the window. He smiled at her as he passed; trying to look like everything was fine and hoping that Paige would be back by the time they returned.

# Chapter 32

He was very well pleased with himself. Things were turning out better than expected. Soon, everything he had planned for, worked for, suffered for would be over. He reveled in his power. He could control his worst enemy. He would soon be able to live his life the way he saw fit. He looked around the dark room with a smile of great accomplishment. He ran his fingers through his hair then placed them on his hips as he continued to survey the room. The sun was bright, he thought, as he glanced toward the boarded window. It cast too much light into the room and that started to make him unhappy. He then realized it was hard to be unhappy on a day like today. The wolves were out now. They were figuring it out, putting the pieces of the puzzle together. Soon, soon it would be over. "Soon you will pay the price for what you have done my little girl," he hissed as he ran his hand across Paige's forehead. He felt the knot that had formed from where he had knocked her out.

Paige's vision had started to return and she looked at him through squinted eyes. He was looking at the window again and not at her. She could see his slim face and his long straight nose. His hair was short.

At least it looked that way to her in the dark light of the room. His eyes looked cold and dark. She could see him smile with perfect white teeth that contrasted with the darkness. He turned toward her and she immediately closed her eyes. She wished she could get a good look at him. She could hear him move about the room and finally heard a door shut.

She slowly opened her eyes again and surveyed what was around her. She could feel the ropes tied around her wrists and remembered being this way once before. This room became familiar all at once. The dark walls were covered with the old velvet wallpaper with Victorian designs. She glanced toward the window and remembered seeing the boards and watching lightning flash, casting shadows across the room.

She turned her head to find the mattress. It was exactly where she remembered and as she remembered with the bloodstains and the long blue and white stripes. She remembered strangling the cats on the mattress. The feeling of total and complete fear took over her as it did all of those months before. Tears began to fall down her cheeks. She licked them off of her mouth, as they were a welcome drink for the thirst she was starting to realize she had. As she tried to turn her head to the wall opposite of the window, she could see a small table with a single brass candlestick and beside that was a chair. Someone was sitting in the chair! She struggled to focus her eyes more, but all she could see was that they were tied up as well. "Junna?" she asked as her vision cleared more. "Junna? Is that really you?"

A soft whimper came from the woman. "Paige?" she whispered.

"Oh, no! He got to you!" Junna began to cry.

"What's going on?" Paige asked looking for some explanation that she hoped Junna had.

144

"If he has you then it's all over. It's all over!" Junna slipped out of consciousness.

"Junna!" Paige tried to say more loudly; afraid the man would overhear her. "Junna, wake up!" After a few tries, Paige gave up.

She listened for signs of anyone else around her. All she could hear were birds chirping outside the window and she could barely see the sun beaming through in streaks across the room. As she tried to move her arms, she could feel the knots tied around her wrists. As she struggled against them, she could hear footsteps as if someone was climbing stairs. She waited until she heard a key slowly unlock the door before the man walked in.

"I see my little pigeon is awake," he seemed to hiss the words has he spoke. Clearly, he was trying to intimidate her. She just looked at him defiantly. "Still trying to be strong; even after all that you have done!

My little pigeon has been a very bad girl," he smiled wickedly at her with his perfect white teeth. Paige still could not see his full face in the darkness.

"What do you want from me?" she demanded.

"I want you to pay for what you have done. Killing three people all by yourself! I will admit Sarah stepping out in front of the bus must have really made you smile. You didn't have to do the dirty deed yourself. My, my, my, you've been very … very … very bad," he taunted her as he rubbed her hair. She tried to pull away from him but was unsuccessful. "Nonetheless, even a bad girl needs to eat." He held a piece of bread in front of her and waved it back and forth before putting it in his own mouth. "See it won't hurt you." He offered her another bite. Paige shook her head.

"Fine, fine. We'll see if my little pigeon wants breadcrumbs later. You need to think about what you have done," he said as he laid the bread on the floor at her feet and turned to walk out.

"What does he mean I killed three people all by myself? I didn't ..." she broke off. "I remember having my hands around Anthony's neck.

I remember the rope in my hands when Richie died. Oh, God! I had a smile on my face in the picture!" She began to thrash in her chair.

"*Get me out of here!*" she screamed. "What have I done?" Tears poured down her face now. "What have I done?" She heaved and vomited on herself. She pulled tightly on the ropes around her wrists and fought against them on her ankles. The chair rocked violently back and forth, but Paige was unable to free herself. "*I want to die. I deserve to die,*" she cried to herself. Exhausted, she realized she couldn't control anything and she finally passed out.

# Chapter 33

John Waters returned to the station, entered his office, plopped down in his chair, and started to think. He hoped that Paige had nothing to do with the murders. That would be absolutely dreadful for his reputation to have a murderer on his force. But, if that were the case, he was determined to figure it all out. If he solved the case and arrested her, he would look like the hero. As he looked around his office, Jones Childers burst in through the door, looking disheveled and exhausted.

Hannah was behind him, trying to prevent him from rushing into John's office.

"Have you found out anything yet?" he asked tearfully.

"No, not yet. Are you sure no one on your farm saw anything?

Nothing at all? No noises or unknown cars?" John asked as he motioned for Jones to sit in a chair across from his desk.

"Not a thing. At least no one has come forward yet. I've asked everyone I can find," Jones began to sob.

John walked over to him and placed his hand on his

shoulder. "I'll call you as soon as we have any idea."

"John, there's one thing I need to tell you. Just in case this helps with anything. Um ... Aileen ... she was having an affair, an affair with David, Paige's boyfriend. Maybe he had something to do with this."

"I'm sorry, Jones. Really I am. We'll do everything we can to find out what happened. I know this is hard. Keep your ears open for anything you can find out. Okay?" John tried to sound sympathetic.

Not feeling any better, Jones stood, shook his hand and left. John felt really sorry for him. He couldn't tell him of the suspicions yet, but this added a motive, at least to Aileen's murder. Maybe he could nail her on that one. He may not be able to pin anything else on her, but he could try to on this one. Paige was missing this morning after all.

*"She was probably at the Childers, having her revenge. But then again, could David be involved? Could he have murdered Aileen? For that matter, could Jones have killed her?"* he thought to himself as he paced around his office.

He walked around his desk. Looking at Paige's office, he decided to go inside and look through her things. She would have to be pretty stupid to leave any evidence around that would implicate her in anything. She's been pretty smart so far. He rummaged through all of the drawers, and all of the papers on her desk. Nothing seemed out of the ordinary. "Hmm," he mumbled. *"The Steckler file. Admiring your own work little girl?"* he thought as he flipped through the file and came across the picture of Paige in the mirror at Anthony's murder.

*"Smiling, I see. Why didn't I notice that before?"* He gathered up the file and headed toward his office to mull it over with the new suspects in his mind.

Jay returned with Harry. He wandered around Paige's

kitchen, looking for any clue, any sign of what was going on. Should he believe Paige? Was she really in need of psychiatric help? Did she really kill anyone? He was so confused. Was Paige using him as her insanity defense or did she honestly believe what she was telling him?

He sat down at the kitchen table and starting going through the stack of mail and newspapers that had piled up over the last few weeks.

He then found the pink envelope. "Junna? Are you for real? Or is that another part of Paige's scheme?" he yelled as he threw the envelope across the room.

*"Paige, if you are a reader, read me now! I don't know what to think. There is so much spinning around in my head. I'm hearing things about you I don't want to know and sure as hell don't want to believe. I don't know what to do. I don't know how to help. And ... where in the hell are you?"* he screamed the words in his mind as if he were trying to let people in China hear him.

He looked in her refrigerator and found a beer and downed the whole thing. Realizing it was only ten o'clock in the morning, he chuckled, grabbed another one and downed it too.

# Chapter 34

Paige sat in the dark room. She was unbelievably exhausted and her head was pounding as if freight trains were running through it.

She still tried to think. She was attempting to remember anything as she thought about Anthony. She could feel her hands around his neck and she remembered as the life drained out of his face and he fell to the floor. She had done it. She killed her sister's husband. Unbelievable pain and grief consumed her. Then she could see as she was helping the very drunken Richie stand on the ladder after putting the rope around his neck. She remembered kicking the ladder out from under him. "My sweet little Richie?" she whispered. Nausea swept over her and she felt faint. "Wait!" she whispered. "He said I killed three? Who was the third? He said Sarah had killed herself. Who is the third?" she questioned as the dizziness took over her senses and her world once again turned black.

She dreamt of Aileen. Aileen was walking out to the barn as she always did early in the morning to check on the horses before anyone else stirred. She felt the weight of the shovel in her hands. "No!" she screamed and woke up.

Junna was watching her, "Paige … Paige … don't let him do this to you!"

"Who? What's he doing to me? I killed them. I killed them all!"

Paige was screaming.

"No … Paige, listen to me. That's not what is happening."

"I felt everything. I saw it happen. I've killed them all!" she screamed at the top of her lungs. Not having any tears left, she didn't know what to think. She just wanted to wake up. These last few months had to be a dream and she needed to wake up from it now. Thoughts of death running through her mind made her believe she needed to die. The world needed to be rid of her filth. What had she done? Why did she do it?

"That's right. You did, you naughty little girl," the deep voice came from the corner by the window. "You will pay for this, my child. You will pay."

"What do you get out of this?" she asked him. "Who are you and what do you want from me? Please, if you want to kill me, do it now. I deserve it. *Just do it now!*" She was getting hoarse from all of the screaming and her words were becoming inaudible.

"All in good time, my child, I will tell you everything. But not now, now you have to suffer a while. You have to pay for all you've done," he said as he stood and crossed the room toward her.

"Leave her alone! Can't you see she's suffered enough? Look at what you've done to her," Junna pleaded.

"Quiet! I'll deal with you later," he yelled at Junna and picked up the bread and threw it at her.

"I'm not afraid of you anymore. Paige, don't listen to him," Junna screamed.

The man stood up and in one swift move, crossed the room and hit Junna in the face, causing her chair to fall over and knocked her unconscious.

"I'm sorry you had to see that dear Paige. She doesn't want to see you suffer like I do. Just look at what you've done. You murdered your *sister's* husband and son. You caused your *sister* to step out in front of the bus. I just wonder what you had in store for her if she hadn't taken care of that little problem for you. Then, you had to knock off your lover's lover. How quaint is that? Tell me, Paige, just why you did it all?" he turned and paced the room. "Aileen I can understand. Oh, wait, the Steckler house. That's what you wanted. You knew it would go to you didn't you?" he laughed uncontrollably. "Hmmm, poor Senator Steckler. It's a good thing he didn't have any family. You would have killed them off too so that you could get what you wanted. Were you really that jealous of Sarah and Anthony's marriage?"

"Who are you?" Paige asked again.

"I told you … all in good time, my little pigeon. All in good time," he laughed as he turned and walked away from Paige.

Paige wished she could see him better. The dark room kept her from seeing much of anything. She wondered why he had such an interest in why she had killed so many. What did he have to do with any of it? She tried to think about him and find him in the collective conscious, but she couldn't concentrate hard enough. All of the pain, both emotional and physical kept her from being able to think clearly.

Her thoughts turned back to the murders. How could she have been capable of killing those she loved most? What else could she be capable of?

He turned back toward her, "I have been watching you most of your life. You've had your perfect little world and you never appreciated any of it. It just wasn't good enough for you, was it?" he paced circles around her, speaking low and evenly. "You never had true love. You are incapable of giving it, so that makes you incapable of getting it and you are jealous of anyone that has it." He cleared his throat and continued, "That's why you did it all isn't it? Jealousy? You had no reason to kill Aileen until David, did you? You couldn't stand anyone else having what you wanted."

Paige was speechless, numb. She felt worthless. She had given up.

"Please, please, just kill me. I deserve it." With that said he raised his hand and hit her across the face. Her world drifted slowly, quietly away from her.

# Chapter 35

John Waters sat down again to review the tapes from Gellendale Estates. As he watched the video, he studied the woman running to and from the house. Her long brown hair was in a ponytail under a black baseball cap. He rewound the video several times and watched each move carefully. He could see her pick up a planter on the porch and throw it through the glass. "Wait!" he said as he backed up the tape once more noticing a last second move on the perpetrators part just before she entered the residence. He watched it again. "Yes, that's it," he rewound it one more time. "That's it! Adam, come here!" he yelled through the station.

A moment later, Adam appeared in the doorway. "Yeah, chief?"

John rewound the tape yet again. "Look at this. Tell me what you see," he showed the tape to Adam three times before he saw it too.

"Her hair fell off! She caught it before it came off completely, but her hair fell off!" Adam declared.

"Thanks, Adam. I just wanted to make sure someone else saw that too."

"No prob, chief." Adam started to walk out of the room but turned toward John, "So the perp didn't have long hair."

John thought about this for a while. Maybe this was someone setting Paige up? Still this was not conclusive proof. Paige had access to the motorcycle. It was next door. It was returned nearby. Or was that too easy? He could understand if the motorcycle were found in the Ohio River but not around the corner. Or was that the way was she wanted it? She's a cop. If things looked too good to be true, that would make it look like a setup and she could try to get off. "She's smart like that," he said out loud. "She could have planned it that way, wig and all. But why?" Just then the thought of the estate went through his mind. Could she have done this to get the house? Why would she kill everyone she had in her life? That just didn't make sense. Or did it? Besides, she already had the house. Why this? Why now?

John walked back and forth. He then replayed the tapes. "*The hair, what's up with the hair?*" he thought as he continued his pacing.

# Chapter 36

Jay felt like he had been hit by a tornado. His whole world was spinning. The cloud of doubt was still hanging low about him. Could Paige be capable of such things? Did she devise the entire plan? Was her memory loss part of the whole thing? And Junna? Did she make her up? Is this all part of an insanity defense to try to get away with murder? What if it is all true? As unbelievable as it seemed, could it all be true?

He paced around the kitchen rubbing his temples. He wanted to believe her. How could he? "Mind reading," he mumbled to himself. "Mind reading? Collective conscious? What the hell is going on?"

In his mad dash from one side of the room to the other, he knocked the newspapers off of the kitchen table. "Shit," he whispered as he bent over to pick them up. As he placed them back on the table, the piece of pink stationery fell out of the pile. He picked it up and read the neat handwriting again.

*Dear Paige Aldridge,*

*I am writing to you because I know what you have been going through. I*

*know about your memories of the dark*
*room. If you want some answers, please*
*think of me when you are alone and I*
*will be there.*

*Junna Breck*

His hands shook as he read the letter over and over. "Okay, Jay. What are you going to do with this one?" he asked as he paced more and continued to read the letter. The phone rang causing him to jump out of his skin.

"Jay Vittadini," he answered.

"Jay, it's Adam. I think we have something."

"Spill it!"

"We can't find a Junna Breck, but we did find a Junna Brooks. She lived here in Louisville at some point."

"How do you know it's the same person?"

"Here's the thing … first of all, how many Junnas could there be?" Adam half chuckled making Jay start to lose his patience. "We found a picture of her in an old edition of the Courier-Journal. As I was looking at it, Hannah looked over my shoulder and recognized her. She said that Junna had dropped off an envelope for Paige just before she came back after Sarah died. I figured it had to be the same person."

A giant wave of relief washed over Jay. It was true! Junna was true at least. This gave Jay some hope. "What was the story about? In the Courier-Journal?"

"Just some story about growing up in The Tree House. Evidently Junna was orphaned or abandoned or something at the age of six. Let me see … nothing too out of the ordinary. Just what life was like there … what food they ate … um … games played … looks like she was helping raise money for the orphanage."

"Anything else?" Jay asked hopefully.

"Not in this? I'm doing a search now on Junna Brooks. We'll see what else that turns up and get you a good address."

"Thanks, man. What about Hannah? Is she there? Can I talk to her?"

"Sure thing. Hold on a sec ..."

Jay waited for the answer. "Hey, Jay," Hannah's cheery voice answered.

"Morning, Hannah. I have a question about Junna Breck, Brooks whatever her name is. What exactly did this Miss Junna drop off for Paige?"

"Only a pink envelope marked Confidential across the back. She just handed it to me and asked that I give it to Paige when she returned.

That's really all I remember."

"Thanks, Hannah. I appreciate your help. Pass me back to Adam, will ya?"

"Sure," she handed the phone to Adam.

"Yeah, Jay?"

"You will let me know as soon as you hear anything ... anything at all?"

"Will do! ... Oh, I was just reviewing the tapes from Gellendale Estates. John had noticed that when the lady was breaking into the house, her hair started to fall off. She caught it just before she entered. Just thought you should know that it looks like our perp didn't have long hair after all."

"Thanks, man. I really appreciate it," Jay took a deep breath and blew it out slowly.

He hung up the phone and ran back to the table. He rummaged through the pile of papers again and found the pink envelope marked Confidential. "Paige, I will help you. Please read me now," he thought.

"I'm on your side. I will help you. I believe in you and I love you. Hang in there, Paige. We'll figure out all of this, together."

# Chapter 37

Paige woke once again. This time, she was in the alley. "What do I do?" she said breathlessly as she stood up, legs shaking. She looked at her wrists. They were bruised and bleeding. She looked at the rope lying at her feet. "I've done this to myself. How long have I been gone this time?" She asked herself as she picked up the rope and started down the alley. She remembered leaving before, almost two years ago. "I have to confess. Turn myself in," she repeated over and over again. As she neared the street, she saw Tom driving by in his cruiser and she flagged him down.

"Jesus Christ, Paige. What's happened to you?" he said as she climbed into the front seat.

"I'll explain it all later. Will you take me to the station?"

"Sure." Tom drove off; neither of them saying a word the whole way.

Paige walked into the station, straight into John Waters' office and shut the door behind her.

After closing his dropped mouth, John asked her to sit.

"I'm here to confess. John, I can't remember everything but I believe I murdered Anthony and Richie Steckler, and now Aileen Childers."

There she said it. It's out there now and she will pay for what she's done.

John's mouth dropped again. "What are you talking about?"

She held up her wrists. "See, I've done this to myself. I've evidently planned to tell you I was kidnapped again."

"You're not making sense. Slow down and start from the beginning,"

John responded in total disbelief.

"This is what I can remember. I strangled Anthony. I remember seeing him die with my hands around his neck. I can see the rope in my hands as I tied it around Richie's neck then kicked the ladder over.

I can feel the shovel in my hands as I hit Aileen. I remember rubbing ropes around my wrists to make them look like this!" Everything spilled out like water from a pitcher. "Lock me up before I do anything else," she begged as tears streamed down her face.

John stood up and walked to her, "Are you sure you want to do this? Your lawyer is not here."

Paige nodded and John helped her stand. He placed the handcuffs carefully around her wrists as he read her rights to her.

As he led her out of his office, the entire station stopped in their tracks to watch. Jay burst through the door as John sat her down in front of Hannah to be booked. She looked up at him and saw the confusion in his face, "I'm sorry, Jay. I'm so sorry."

"What's this all about?" Jay demanded of John. "You have no proof!"

"Jay, calm down. She's come in on her own. She's confessed to all three murders."

"What?" puzzled, he sat immediately down in a chair next to Paige.

"What are you doing?"

Paige struggled to speak. "I remember things. Things I shouldn't remember. Jay, I remember killing them all and I don't know why I did it!"

"I have to lock her up, Jay." John placed his hand on Jay's shoulder.

The look of disbelief on his face matched that of Jay's. Hannah had not yet moved.

"Paige, couldn't you hear me? Couldn't you hear me tell you I believe you? I'm on your side, Paige. Couldn't you hear me?" Jay was pleading with her.

"No, no. What are you talking about?" she whispered as she looked at him with a puzzled expression.

"Junna. I found some info on Junna," Jay said desperately trying to snap Paige out of it.

"Who's Junna?" she asked blankly.

John butted in, "Yeah, who's Junna?"

"What do you mean?" Jay begged. "Junna, Junna Breck. I think we've found her."

Paige just looked away. She didn't have tears to cry. What did Junna have to do with this? Paige felt as if she were sinking, sinking through her chair, through the floor. Her head was spinning. Guilt and grief had completely consumed her. She would rather die than to face another day.

She could hear the muffled conversations around her. She could tell people were walking by and looking at her, but she couldn't understand a thing they were saying or what they were doing. It was all noise. She felt as if she was in the middle of a whirlwind and the entire world was whizzing around her so rapidly that she couldn't make anything out of it. She wanted to pay. She had been bad, very bad and she wanted to pay. She could hear a voice talking in her head, telling her how bad she was. Then she could hear another voice telling her not to listen. Not to believe anything that was happening to her. She barely felt Jay touch her hand. She wanted to pull away but was unable to move. Someone helped her stand and walk. Where were they going? She didn't know; didn't care.

# Chapter 38

Adam couldn't believe his eyes. He found Junna. There was a second article in the Courier-Journal about her. Junna Brooks was abandoned along with two other siblings. An older brother named Shepherd and a younger sister named Glenna. Junna and Shepherd were not adopted and had to grow up in The Tree House. After running away for a period of three months, Junna returned alone. Ian Messing had helped raise her at the Orphanage for a while but Junna Brooks was sent to a foster family and there was no sign of her since then. She simply just disappeared.

Adam looked up from the computer and saw Jay sitting next to the chair where Paige had been. "What on earth is going on?" he walked out as Paige was led away in handcuffs.

"I need to talk to you," Jay pulled Adam by his arm and led him back into Adam's office.

"Have you found out anything … anything at all about Junna?"

"Yes," Adam explained the article.

"Do you have an address of the foster home?" Jay

questioned.

"Well of course. We do have that information." Adam held up a piece of paper that he jotted the information on.

"I'm going to talk to them now," Jay grabbed the paper and headed out the door. He read the address as he jumped into his car. "Mr. and Mrs. Brett Logins, Henry County? This is in Henry County!" He started the car and sped away.

The drive was long and slow due to construction on I-71. Jay turned on his siren and went around them all in the emergency lane. He sped along as much as possible being impatient with everyone on the road.

"Idiots!" he screamed, as people would not move out of his way.

When he arrived at the address, he ran up and knocked on the door.

A small elderly woman opened the door. She was in her housecoat and was carrying a cup of coffee.

Jay showed her his badge and asked if he could ask some questions.

"Okay, but please sit down on the swing," she gestured toward an old swing that was in bad need of repainting. "Would you like something to drink?"

"No, I'm fine." He forced a smile at her. "I need to ask you about Junna Brooks. Have you seen her lately?"

"No, not for a while. She left here several years ago. Sweet girl. I really thought of her as my daughter. I don't know what happened to her. Is she alright? I've waited so long to hear from her. I never thought she would do this to me. I've been so worried."

"I don't know. I've never met her. But I would like to. If she comes by would you tell her to give me a call?" he said as he smiled at her again and handed her his card.

"What about your husband, would he know anything?"

"No, no. He passed away five years back. I've had a heck of a time keeping this farm running without him. I've hired a man to run it for me, but he just doesn't do it the way poor Brett used to. He stays out back. We have another small house. It used to be a slave house. I don't think of him as a slave, just some help. Don't get me wrong, he does a great job. It just will never compare to my poor Brett, God rest his soul," Mrs. Logins rambled on. "It's hard keeping up with the fields.

We gave up on corn. It's all soybeans now. You know, he asked about her before. About Junna. Said he knew her a few years back. I figured he was sweet on her. She is a little beauty."

"Wait," Jay interrupted. "He knows Junna? Is he around? I'd like to talk to him too."

"He comes and goes. Don't know if he's here right now, but he lives in the house in the back. Just drive around the side there," she pointed to a small gravel road that went around the house. "You can't miss it. It's the only thing that's not a barn back there."

"Thank you, Mrs. Logins. You've been a great help. If you hear from Junna, please let me know," he said as he shook her hand lightly and left, heading for the house in the back.

Jay parked along a chain link fence that lined the driveway. The house sat on a steep hill with weeds and grass grown up all around. He knocked several times before trying the handle. The door was not locked. As he entered the door, he stepped into a huge kitchen with wooden floors and wooden counter tops. Off to the left was a small, sunken room that was set up for watching television. To the right was a large living room. Behind that was a sitting area that had an upright piano in the corner. The walls of this room were painted an awful lime green.

Jay walked through the living room and into a large

bedroom. There was nothing special about this room. It was painted a dull white and the bed was covered with a well-used quilt. He looked around the room for a sign of who lived there. There were no clothes, shoes, no clues at all.

He passed through the bedroom into a large bathroom. The bathroom was large enough to include a king sized bed. The bed was covered in a purple flowered bedspread and beside it sat a small garbage can full of tissues. To the left was a door that was lined with purple curtains. He slid the slide bolt lock to the side to try to open the door, but it wouldn't open easily. After a good push, it opened to reveal old open wooden stairs.

The stairway was very dusty, but he could see where footprints were made proving someone had recently passed over them. He cautiously climbed the stairs and made his way to the top. He walked into the room that looked like a mezzanine over a sawmill. There were windows that lined all around and cabinets that were trimmed in copper. He looked out over the sawmill at the equipment that he could tell had been unused for quite a long time. He walked around the room until he found another door that has locked with a slide bolt. As he touched the bolt, he heard a woman scream.

He listened carefully. "Hello?" he yelled.

He again heard a woman's voice. "Hello! Oh God help me!"

Jay tried to open the door. "Locked!" he screamed as he busted through. "Where are you?"

"I'm here! I'm here!" He followed the voice up another flight of stairs. When he came to a closed door, he knocked it down to get into the room where the screams were coming from.

"Thank God. Thank God!" she was crying hysterically. Jay ran to her. She was tied to a chair and was beaten severely. He cut her loose and helped her to her feet. As she sobbed on his shoulder, he looked around the room. He could see a boarded window, just as Paige had described it. He found the mattress; the bloody mattress.

"You're Junna!" he said as the reality of the situation sank in.

"Yes. How did you know? How did you find me?"

"I'm a friend of Paige's. She needs your help."

"I know, she's confessed. Get me out of here first. He could be back any second."

"Who?" Jay questioned.

"I'll explain later. First we have to help Paige." Jay picked her up and carried her to the car.

# Chapter 39

*"No!"* the man screamed in the middle of Pauline's Restaurant. Realizing he yelled out loud, he looked around the café and then at the newspaper in his hand. "My team lost. Darn those Cardinals" he pretended to laugh it off as the crowd just looked at him as if he were nuts. He threw money on the table and ran out of the café. Why didn't he think of Jay? He hadn't expected Jay to be so smart. He was reading him. He knew he had Junna and he couldn't get to the farm quick enough to stop them. "The police station, they are going to the police station," he said out loud just in case Junna was trying to read him. He had to be more careful to block her out. He ran to his pickup truck and headed toward the police station.

He parked across the street and started to concentrate. He could read Jay's thoughts and started to interject his own. Jay was thinking about how to get the police chief to listen to him and to Junna. Jay thought it was crazy to believe he could convince John about the reading. "Think Jay," he said icily. "It is crazy. Junna is just as crazy. She's messing with everyone. She's not on your side. Paige is guilty. She and Junna are in it together. This is all a cover up."

Meanwhile, Jay looked over at Junna, who was staring straight ahead but not focused on anything. "She's crazy," he thought. "She's helping Paige cover this up. It's an insanity defense for them both. They are both guilty."

Suddenly, Junna turned toward him. "Jay, don't let him do this. You know what you believe. Don't let him in. He's trying to turn you against us all."

Jay blinked at her nervously, "You read me?"

"Yes. I read you and your thoughts were not your own. Who do you believe, Jay?"

Jay shook his head as if clearing cobwebs from his brain. "I believe in Paige," he sighed.

"Good, now let's get to her. Keep your mind focused on only your belief in her."

They didn't speak another word until they arrived at the police station. A crowd had gathered around the area to protest the arrest of a juvenile. At least that was what Jay could make out of the noise of the crowd as they fought their way through. Once inside, Jay looked for John. He found Hannah and asked her to get something for Junna to drink. He grabbed Adam by the arm and ran to John's office.

# Chapter 40

Paige woke cold and hungry. She looked around to find that she was in a dark room. This one was lined with bars. She realized where she was. All of the grief of what she had done suddenly sat on her chest, making it impossible to breathe.

She heard a door open and footsteps heading her way. She saw Jay first. Someone was behind him, but she couldn't see who it was until Junna stepped around. Paige knew she looked familiar and within a few seconds, she remembered her.

"What's going on Junna? Please tell me."

"He'll kill me if I do, but I'm dead anyway. Please try to block him. I know you are weak right now, but try really hard to block him," Junna pleaded.

Paige nodded as Jay opened the cell and they both walked in to sit on the cot in the corner of the room. John Waters walked in behind them and Adam behind him. They stood guarding the doorway.

"Where do I start?" Junna started coughing uncontrollably. After she had cleared her throat, she began again. "When I was six, my mother died and my father left me on the doorstep of The Tree House. I was not alone. I had a four-year-old brother and a three-year old-sister ..." she hesitated a moment. "I'll come back to that one. My sister was lucky enough to be adopted right away. Shepherd and I were never adopted and had to live in The Tree House until I was sixteen. Ian Messing was cruel and uncaring. Life was unbearable there for us so I ran away taking my younger brother with me."

Paige looked around the room. She wanted Jay to look at her, but he just stared at the door.

Junna continued, "Anyway, we found an abandoned farm house not far from the orphanage, broke in and stayed there. My brother was fourteen then and was as impossible as a fourteen-year-old could be. At least that's what I thought that was it. I moved into the main house with the couple. They told me I could be their daughter and stay with them so we went through the foster program. But I kept my brother hidden in the house. He was a bit unique. I know this is sounding all mixed up, but I don't know how to explain it all, especially in a rush," Junna began to cry.

Paige started to think about what this had to do with her and quickly remembered the shovel in her hand, watching Aileen. She lost her train of thought completely.

"My brother started behaving even more strangely one day. He seemed to have eyes in the back of his head where I was concerned. He always showed up as soon as I had whatever dinner I could scrounge up. He seemed to always know what I was thinking. I soon figured it out and I figured out how to stop him. I figured out he had a gift and I had it too. I had to hide it from him. He was becoming controlling and mean. Abusive ... so abusive. He thought of his gift as power and he used it as such. I learned to control my thoughts so I could avoid him; to deceive him. He didn't seem to catch on to what I was doing so I got away and went back to the orphanage. I didn't see him again."

Paige was beginning to understand. It was becoming harder to concentrate on the deaths of her friends and what Junna was telling her so she pulled on her arm causing excruciating pain. She had to think about the pain.

Junna waited for Paige to catch her breath. Jay, Tom, and Adam watched in disbelief.

"I kept up with you, Paige. That was my fault. I helped him find you. I remembered the couple that came in to adopt you and their young daughter, Sarah. I remembered everything. I was hurt that it wasn't me, but Shepherd, my brother, was devastated. He hated the life you had while we were in that awful orphanage."

Paige began to cry. "You're my sister. That evil man is my brother!"

"He had to fight to survive after I left him and went back to the orphanage. God only knows what has happened to him. Whatever it was only made him stronger. I'm sure he used his gift to convince people to give him what he wanted. Now he wants you to pay. Pay for the crimes he's done," she paused before she continued. "He has always hated you. From the time you were adopted, he hated you and the family that took care of you. I can't say that I didn't feel some resentment, but I truly was happy for you. When you disappeared, I knew what happened. I could read you. I knew. I saw what you were thinking, but I couldn't find you. I had no idea you were here. Maybe he blocked that from me. I couldn't read you again until it was too late. I never gave up. I kept trying until one day I could read your thoughts. You were trying to help Sarah. But it was too late. I finally found Shepherd in the collective conscious and knew what he had done. The search for the two of you was making me more powerful. He knows that now and that's why I am here. He found me. He found my house and waited for me and took me to that awful place. Paige, you didn't kill anyone. He did. He did it and is somehow transferring his memories and thoughts to you as if you did everything. He's trying to get you to admit to killing all of them. That's his plan. Have faith in yourself, Paige. I hope I haven't done you more harm by telling you. But you need to know. It wasn't you! You need to fight him."

John interrupted, "Jay, this is what you wanted me to hear? This is nuts and you are going along with it! Out, all of you, out!"

Jay took Paige's hand, "Read me, Paige."

She looked at him and shut her eyes. She opened them and looked at him. She could hear him say, "Paige, I love you. I believe in you. Believe in yourself too."

He kissed Paige softly on the forehead and took Junna by the arm and led her out. Junna turned to Paige, "He's right, you know."

# Chapter 41

Paige sat in silence in the cell. She closed her eyes. *"I don't care if you can read me, Shepherd. I know who you are and what you are up to. I may be in this cell now, but I won't be for long. I believe in Jay and I believe in Junna. They will convince everyone of what you did. You won't pin this on me."* She paced around the cell, still thinking in her head. *"Hear me now, Shepherd. You will not control my thoughts any longer. It's not my fault. I don't know why I was chosen for adoption, but it is not my fault. I don't know what has happened to you, but you will not defeat me. Not while there is a breath left in my body!"*

She could hear the icy voice, *"You have no idea what I can do, dear pigeon. You may be getting stronger, but your friends aren't. No one will believe you. They all will think you are crazy. After all, you are crazy. You've imagined everything, dear pigeon. Everything. See, you are hearing voices. You are crazy. Just wait and see."*

Tears swelled up in her eyes again. Paige sat down on the cot and curled up into a ball to rock back and forth. *"Is it true? Have I gone crazy? Have I imagined everything?"* As she rocked back and forth, John Waters watched her from down the hall, wondering the same thing.

Jay and Junna headed out to the Steckler Estate. "There has to be something. Some shred of evidence that Shepherd was here," Jay said to Junna as they got out of the car and headed toward the broken door.

Jay pushed the yellow tape aside and entered the foyer. They wandered around the room looking for any sign of evidence.

"I never thought I'd set foot in here," Junna whispered as she walked up behind Jay. "I've seen it from the outside so many times when I'd drive by trying to catch a glimpse of my sister."

Jay touched her arm, "I'm sorry. I know that must have been very hard for you being able to see your sister and not being able to talk to her."

"I did what I had to, or thought I had to," Junna sighed and continued to look around. She stopped in her tracks when she finally saw the writing in red on the wall. "My brother is also very stupid. Did he really think this would lead the police to Paige?"

"I guess he thought it might if we were to believe this to be a warning."

Junna nodded and continued to look around the estate, which was now empty from the auction.

Suddenly a voice came from the hall, "Hello, Jay. You here?" It was John Waters.

Jay walked back toward the front door. John reached out his hand to Jay but Jay didn't take it.

"I want to apologize. I should not have behaved the way I did earlier.

In fact," he looked over his shoulder as Paige walked through the door, "I decided to give her the benefit of the doubt. Something kept telling me to trust Paige."

Paige glanced at Junna, who passed her a quick smile

and a wink making Paige smile as well.

John continued, "She's still in custody with me. But I thought maybe her being here would jog a memory or help us out some way."

"That's a great idea," Jay beamed as he hugged Paige.

Paige slowly walked around the room. She rubbed her hand along the paint and tried to envision what had happened here. She then walked out to the garage. It was all she could do to keep any composure possible as she remembered the rope in her hands and watching Richie swing from the rafters. "Why did he have to do this to us?" she said out loud.

The others joined her in the garage. They watched her walk around in circles, whispering her thoughts so that no one else could hear.

"Good, you are all here," an icy voice came from the doorway. "I would like for you all to move to the corner where I can see you clearly, with your hands up, of course." The man moved into the light. Everyone saw that he had two handguns, resembling a gunfighter, pointed at them all. "And don't bother thinking about reaching for your own guns. I will know it before you do. I can read minds you know."

They all gathered in the corner of the garage. Jay placed his arms around both Paige and Junna while John stood beside them. Shepherd walked up to them, running the barrel of one handgun along Paige's cheek. "After today, my life will be complete. You will all have paid for the crimes committed against me. *All of you!*" he screamed in Junna's face.

"What happened to you, Shepherd?" Junna asked him. "Let me know why you are doing this? Why do we need to die?"

"Sweet little, Junna. Do you not remember? Or do you choose to forget?" He then ran the barrel down her cheek. "Old man Messing, remember him?" He backed away and looked at the rest of the group.

"I know Junna has let you all in on our little secret. That's why you all have to die."

"What about old man Messing?" Junna interrupted.

He moved quickly back to her face, keeping his guns pointed at her and Paige. "I'll deal with him soon. You don't know what it's like to read the mind of a very, very sick man, do you? You never tried! You didn't hear night after night how that man wanted to touch us, smell us, rape us. Over and over I listened to him. I knew every one of that sick man's fantasies. I watched them all come true. All the while, our perfect little sister was living happily ever after in her fairy tale land. Oblivious to all that we were going through! Being loved by these horrid little rich bastards! And then you, my dear Junna, had to go and try to raise money to keep that damn place open!" He started to pace around the room.

Jay pulled the girls closer to him. Paige could feel his gun push into her side. She started whispering the words "Don't think. Don't think. Feel the gun. Reach for the gun." While tying to think, *"Be still, don't move".*

Shepherd continued his rant. "Paige, you were so easy to suggest to. You were so easy to find thinking about you dear dead friends. It was so easy for me to interrupt your thoughts and dreams with *my* memories, especially when you were mine when I kept you in that dark place, getting into your head, infiltrating your dreams," he laughed. "It was so easy to convince you that you killed everyone. My God, you are so weak, so vulnerable. I think I could have convinced you that you shot President Lincoln. I even had you believing you had killed cats with your bare hands! It was such pleasure to cause you grief! You cared so much for your family, but you were still so lonely. You still wanted more, you selfish little bitch. It was so easy to convince you that you killed everyone out of jealousy. So easy to convince you that you were losing your mind."

As soon as he said the last word an explosion reverberated through the garage. Two more shots were fired; one, hitting Junna in the leg and the other hitting the garage door. The first, however, hit its mark.

Shepherd sank slowly to the floor, dropping both guns. Jay hurried and kicked them out of reach.

"How?" Shepherd asked as he fell to the floor.

"You're not the only one with a gift," Paige smiled at him while still holding Jay's gun. "You thought I was afraid. You thought I was telling myself to keep very still. At least, that's what I wanted you to think. You believed what I wanted you to believe, Shepherd. How does that feel?" she said as she watched him slowly drift away.

# Chapter 42

The next week was extremely busy. John and Jay were trying to keep everything out of the press with the exception of the fact that the murderer had been caught and was killed in self-defense. Paige and Junna were spending time getting to know one another and becoming fast friends while helping each other recover.

The two of them were sitting at a small table in Pauline's when Jay walked in.

"Hey ladies," he smiled and kissed Paige as he sat down. "Paige, Junna, I have something to tell you. I just found out myself."

"What's that?" Paige smiled up and him.

"I just spoke with John Waters. It seems he's had a secret," Paige resisted the urge to read him. "It appears Mr. Messing has been arrested for a running prostitution ring as well as possession of child pornography."

Paige couldn't believe her ears. "I knew that chick I saw him with was a whore!" Paige remembered seeing Ian in the restaurant while having dinner with David.

Junna reached across the table and took her hand.

"That's just perfect! He'll no doubt use the estate

money for all of his legal fees," Junna sighed.

"I'll make sure that doesn't happen," Paige said lightly.

"Yeah, all the money will be spent on the kids, and on finding a new Ian Messing." Jay stood up from the table and looked at Paige.

Paige jumped into his arms and kissed him happily, "Now all we have to do is find a way to prosecute him for his abuse. At least he will not be around to harm anyone else. We all are witnesses to Shepherd's confession. Others should come out now." She turned and hugged Junna.

"Excuse me," a voice sounded from behind. "Are you Paige Aldridge?"

Paige turned to find two gentlemen in suits looking at them.

"Yes," she replied looking puzzled.

"You must be Junna Brooks?" One of them asked.

"Yes," Junna responded with the same puzzled look.

"My we speak with the two of you outside?" he gestured his arm to point them toward the door.

"Sure," Paige replied as they started to follow, leaving Jay behind.

She tried to read them as they were walking out the door, but she could not find them in the collective conscious in such a short amount of time. She looked at Junna and could tell that she was doing the same thing. After reaching the alley, he took out his badge.

"I'm Special Agent Aaron Caldwell and this is Special Agent Albert Morgan with the FBI, ma'am," he said as he looked at Paige. "We are here to talk to you both about working for us."

**END**

## About Lynn Tincher

Lynn studied Theater Arts in College in hopes of becoming a Drama/English teacher. She has written articles in local newspapers and travel brochures. Now, she is focused on writing novels, short stories, articles and poems. She also visits schools and writer's groups to help encourage other writers.

Not only does Lynn look forward to sharing her stories, she is also focused on helping other new writers in their efforts to get published. Visit Lynn's website at http://www.lynntincher.com/ and you may contact her at lynntincher@me.com. She is also the Louisville Creative Writing Examiner on Examiner.

Her inspiration comes from some of her favorite authors, Robert Powell, Nora Roberts, Piers Anthony and J.K. Rowling. (Yes, she's a Potter fan!)

In September of 2010, Lynn was diagnosed with Brugada Syndrome, a rare and fatal genetic heart disease. She is determined to help spread the word about Brugada Syndrome and hopes to help others who are dealing with it.

Lynn now lives in Prospect, Kentucky with her husband. She has three wonderful children, Emily, Aaron and Becca and two fantastic dogs named Luke and Mara.

*Afterthoughts*

CPSIA information can be obtained
at www.ICGtesting.com
Printed in the USA
FFOW01n1108220516
24172FF

9 781942 212218